"As tempting as that might be," Declan told her, **"I'm speaking as the primary on this case, not as someone who's attracted to you."**

Charley's eyes widened. Was that another slip of the tongue? Or…? "Are you?" she heard herself asking. At least, it sounded like her voice, although for the life of her, Charley couldn't have said where her question had come from.

The parking lot was deserted. The skeleton crew that was on duty had found parking in the front of the building. There was no one else in the immediate vicinity, no vehicles passing by. No one, he was acutely aware, to see them.

"No," Declan answered, threading his fingers through her hair just before he cupped the back of Charley's head. The words slipped from his lips in a hushed breath before he lowered his mouth to hers and did what he realized he'd been wanting to do since the first time he'd laid eyes on her seven years ago.

CAVANAUGH HERO

BY
MARIE FERRARELLA

~~All rights reserved including the right of reproduction in whole or in part in any form. This edition is published by arrangement with Harlequin Books S.A.~~

~~This book is sold subject to the condition that it shall not, by way of trade or otherwise, be lent, resold, hired out or otherwise circulated without the prior consent of the publisher in any form of binding or cover other than that in which it is published and without a similar condition including this condition being imposed on the subsequent purchaser.~~

~~This is a work of fiction. Names, characters, places, locations and incidents are purely fictional and bear no relationship to any real life individuals, living or dead, or to any actual places, business establishments, locations, events or incidents. Any resemblance is entirely coincidental.~~

Published in Great Britain 2014
by Mills & Boon, an imprint of Harlequin (UK) Limited,
Eton House, 18-24 Paradise Road, Richmond, Surrey, TW9 1SR

© 2014 Marie Rydzynski-Ferrarella

ISBN: 978 0 263 91418 4

18-0214

Harlequin (UK) Limited's policy is to use papers that are natural, renewable and rec̶y̶c̶l̶a̶b̶l̶e̶ ̶p̶r̶o̶d̶u̶c̶t̶s̶ ̶a̶n̶d̶ ̶m̶a̶d̶e̶ ̶f̶r̶o̶m̶ ̶w̶o̶o̶d̶ ̶g̶r̶o̶w̶n̶ ̶i̶n̶ ̶s̶u̶s̶t̶a̶i̶n̶a̶b̶l̶e̶ forests.
The log̶g̶i̶n̶g̶ ̶a̶n̶d̶ ̶m̶a̶n̶u̶f̶a̶c̶t̶u̶r̶i̶n̶g̶ ̶p̶r̶o̶c̶e̶s̶s̶e̶s̶ ̶c̶o̶n̶f̶o̶r̶m̶ ̶t̶o̶ ̶t̶h̶e̶ ̶l̶e̶g̶a̶l̶ ̶e̶n̶v̶i̶r̶o̶n̶mental
regulati̶o̶n̶s̶ ̶o̶f̶ ̶t̶h̶e̶ ̶c̶o̶u̶n̶t̶r̶y̶ ̶o̶f̶ ̶o̶r̶i̶g̶i̶n̶.̶

Printed ̶a̶n̶d̶ ̶b̶o̶u̶n̶d̶ ̶i̶n̶ ̶S̶p̶a̶i̶n̶
by Blac̶k̶p̶r̶i̶n̶t̶ ̶C̶P̶I̶,̶ ̶B̶a̶r̶c̶e̶l̶o̶n̶a̶

A *USA TODAY* bestselling and RITA® Award-winning author, **Marie Ferrarella** has written more than two hundred books for Mills & Boon, some under the name Marie Nicole. Her romances are beloved by fans worldwide. Visit her website, www.marieferrarella.com.

To all the readers who have been following
the Cavanaughs since the first book and
have asked for more.

Prologue

The gunshot was muffled deliberately, the extension on the end of the gun barrel all but silencing the scream of the bullet. A bullet that ended a life in less than a heartbeat.

One minute the inebriated, off-duty police officer on the sofa was looking up with those pathetic, puppy-dog eyes, talking about some little two-bit who had strung him along; the next, he wasn't talking at all and those puppy-dog eyes weren't looking at anything anymore.

The cop never knew what hit him, the shooter thought with satisfaction. He certainly hadn't been expecting it, which was the whole point. The liquor had done its job, lulling the cop into a sense of complacency.

The shooter relished every millisecond of the bullet's flight upon release. Relished even more the irreversible damage done by that bullet once it buried itself in the intended target's flesh.

The shooter watched in captivated fascination as the last bit of light—and life—left Sergeant Matthew Holt's gray eyes.

And within the shooter's head, the sound of the discharging weapon had roared its presence, declaring its mission to be accomplished.

Justice.

Nothing short of justice had been carried out. A death had been avenged.

Vengeance doesn't only belong to God, but to me, as well.

"That'll teach you," the shooter said, addressing the blue-clad man on the sofa, the man with opened eyes that could no longer see.

The smile widened along the thin lips, a smile that not only represented triumph over what had just happened, but also saw into the future and relished the deaths that were to be.

"Don't worry," the shooter said to the dead man who lay sprawled on his once-white sectional sofa. "You're not going to be alone for long. You'll have a whole lot of company before I'm through."

The cold, heartless smile spread even wider in

barely contained anticipation. That was all there was left to live for these days.

Anticipation.

And revenge.

"Might even get crowded up there before I'm through."

The shooter laughed, envisioning the carnage. And then, just as suddenly, the laughter ceased, vanishing as if it had never existed at all.

Sergeant Holt's executioner took out an eight-by-ten sheet of paper that had carefully cut-out letters pasted on it, pristine letters that didn't have even a smudge of fingerprints on them, thanks to the disposable plastic gloves on the shooter's hands. The gloves were as antiseptic as any that were hospital-issued.

Holding the sheet of paper, the shooter bent over the still man, careful not to step in any of the blood that was even now spilling out onto the floor directly below the body, pooling there at a mesmerizing pace.

The paper kept slipping off the body.

"Damn it," the shooter snapped, swallowing a more ripe curse. The paper was supposed to stay on Holt's chest. The chest that was no longer moving, no longer drawing breath.

How the hell—?

And then, just like that, there was an answer.

The shooter rose, picked up a stapler off the victim's desk and returned to the body. Leaning over the man who could no longer feel anything, the shooter stapled the note to his chest.

"Now it won't slip off," the shooter announced in triumph, laughing again, the sound a sharp contrast to the still body on the bloodied sectional next to the coffee table.

Dark brown eyes squinted as a mocking expression slipped over the shooter's face. "Too bad you can't put this lesson to any use."

Standing back, the shooter admired the sign stapled to the victim's chest. In a flurry of uneven, mismatched letters, the note made a chilling promise: "Only the beginning."

The shooter paused for a few more seconds to admire the scene. There was an intense, overwhelming desire to smash the victim's face in, but the shooter refrained from acting on it. Nothing could be allowed to mute the force of the message and if the victim's face was obliterated, the power of the message might be lost. Because Holt was the first offender—but he was definitely not the last. Not by a very long shot.

"You brought this on yourself" were the last words the shooter uttered before quietly slipping out of the house and into the darkness of a moonless night.

The door was left unlocked, inviting discovery. And soon.

Chapter 1

She did what she could to keep the concern out of her voice, even though it steadily increased with every mile she drove.

"Look, I know that Melissa ripped out your heart, but the best revenge is living well, remember? You taught me that. You said you have to pick yourself up, dust yourself off and start all over again. And if you don't get your butt in gear, big brother, I *will* sing the rest of that song and we all know how well I can carry a tune—but if I have to, I will and you'll only have yourself to blame if your ears fall off."

Holding her breath, she flew through the intersection, just as the light was turning red. It wasn't the best way for a police detective to act, but she couldn't shake the sense of urgency squeezing her chest more and more tightly.

"Seriously, Matt, I'm worried about you. It's not like you not to show up at work for two days in a row—and not even call with an excuse that a four-year-old could see through. I know the bottle has had a certain anesthetizing allure for you lately, but you've been restricting it to nights when you don't have work the next day. This is a giant leap forward for you and it's *not* a good one."

She sighed, searching for something reassuring to say.

"Look at it this way, at least you found out now, before you married her. What if you *had* married her? What if there were kids in the mix? 'Member how bad it was for us when the old man split and Mom got all flaky before *she* cut out on us, too? We survived that, right? We—you," she corrected herself, "will survive this, too. And this time, *you* can lean on me. It's about time that I paid you back for all your support. I know that I owe you big-time."

Detective Charlotte Randolph—Charley to everyone who knew her—had kept up a steady stream of chatter on her cell phone via the Bluetooth piece attached to her ear for the past fifteen minutes in an attempt to deny that she really was in a high state of agitation. Sergeant Matthew Holt hadn't shown up for work or called in for the past two days, neither of which were even *close* to standard behavior for the police officer.

Matt was her older half brother, a fact that they had both kept quiet. Matt's reason was because he wanted her to succeed on her own, without any possible fallout—good or bad—that might come her way because she was related to him. He wanted there to be no question that any success she achieved was hers alone.

Charley went along with the secrecy only because where Matt was concerned, she had a very soft spot in her heart and he could ask her to do anything.

If not for him putting his life on hold when their mother had taken off like that, Charley was certain things in her life might have turned out very differently. For one thing, she would have been swallowed up by the system for three years. She was fifteen and Matt eighteen when Maura Allen Holt Randolph took off with the latest man in her life, leaving behind two offspring without so much as a goodbye note. Certainly not with any money other than what Matt had in the pocket of his jeans, money he'd earned working part-time in a hardware store after school. Their mother had even taken the small amount Matt had hidden in his shoe in the back of his closet. Maura's credo was what was hers was hers and what was yours was hers if she could find it. She was very good at finding things, Charley thought.

For the most part, Matt had raised himself and when she had come along three years later, he had raised her, as well. On the whole, he was far more enchanted with the baby sister he was charged with watching than the woman who had given birth to her. Maura made it a point to tell them more than once that there was "always more where you came from," making sure that neither one of them felt they were special in any way.

But Matt had gone out of his way to make her feel as if she *was* special, Charley recalled now with a fond smile. It was Matt who remembered her birthday and always found *something* to give her, no matter how small a gift it might seem. Like the year he found a doll someone had thrown out in the Dumpster in the alley behind their building. He'd spent days cleaning it up, making it into a presentable doll to give her. He even managed to sew up—awkwardly—the rips in Mattie's dress.

That was what she'd called the doll. Mattie. After her brother.

And she still had it, perched on the upper shelf in her closet. It was a constant tangible reminder of her brother's love.

Matthew was the reason behind almost everything she did. She'd joined the police force because that was the career that Matt had picked for himself. She would have gladly followed him to hell and back if that was the path he'd settled on, but the Aurora Police Department turned out to be the career choice for him—which was just fine with her.

And then Matt fell for Melissa. Hard. Like the proverbial ton of bricks. When he did, she had psyched herself up to accept second place in her brother's life, thrilled that he had found someone to love. That he was finally going to have time to do all the normal things: get married, have kids, buy a house and experience the wonderfully mundane life they'd never had while growing up.

Except, Charley now thought bitterly, that the woman her brother had fallen for so terribly hard had an icicle in place of a heart. Once the novelty of their relationship had worn off for her, Melissa thought nothing of stepping out on Matt.

She took everything he had to offer her—gifts, money as well as his undying love—and then broke off their relationship, grinding his feelings into the dust as if they were no more than bothersome gnats.

Matt never knew what hit him, never knew what he had done wrong. And even though she kept trying to make her brother see that the fault was not with him but with Melissa, nothing she could do or say could help her get through to him.

That was when the drinking started.

And apparently, it still hadn't stopped even though he'd promised her that it had, that he had taken his last drink, wasted his last hour mourning the loss of Melissa.

"I won't let that little two-bit ruin you," Charley declared fiercely, her voice echoing back within the white sedan she drove. "You're too good for her and you know it!" she cried, all but shouting the words into the cell phone that was mounted on her dashboard.

A second later, she was finally pulling into the driveway of the modest two-story house Matt had bought in hopes of bringing Melissa here and starting a family with her.

To Charley's way of thinking, the house had dodged a bullet—and so had Matt. Now all she had to do was make her brother see it. She could be extremely persuasive when she had to be but this, she knew, was going to take every single trick she had in the proverbial book—and maybe even more than that.

Putting the sedan into Park, Charley ended her call, tucked the cell into her pocket and got out of the car. She pressed her lips together as she surveyed the front of the house.

"I swear I don't know what I'll do if I find you on the floor, sleeping off a bender," she muttered to both herself and the brother who wasn't there.

Charley fished out the spare key that Matt had given her but found that she had no need of it. Not only was the front door unlocked, it was standing slightly ajar, as well.

"Well, this is a new low in carelessness for you. Are you daring the neighborhood thief to come in and ransack the place—or *think* he can do it only to have you get the drop on him? Are you really that hard up for entertainment?" she asked.

Charley lightly made contact with the door and pushed it a fraction at a time until the door was open all the way off to one side.

"Matt?" she called out hesitantly. "Are you in there? Matt, it's me, Charley. I elected myself to drag your sorry butt in to work before your lieutenant gets it into his head to fire you and you decide you have no choice but to move in with me. You know you'll just wind up cramping my style."

Not that she had anything that would have remotely passed for something as structured as a "style." Charley was far too busy these days trying to work her way up the ladder, trying to make something of herself within the department.

Trying to, she secretly admitted, to make Matt proud of her.

Because they were both part of the police force, someone might have thought that Matt and she were in competition with one another, but nothing could be farther from the truth. Matt and she had always been a team, a smooth-running, entirely supportive team. If there were shots to be called, she always let Matt call them.

Quite simply, unlike most brothers and sisters, Charley adored the ground Matt walked on and she knew the reverse was true as well, even if he never said as much. He didn't have to. His actions spoke louder than any words.

Matt was her rock.

Which was why seeing him this way, consumed with sorrow because of a woman so unequal to even the dirt beneath his fingernails was just killing her. She didn't know how to snap him out of it. She only knew she had to—because he'd obviously had a relapse.

"Matt?" she called out again, feeling her heart constrict when she didn't receive an answer. "Are you here? You'd better be, otherwise leaving this door unlocked was a really stupid move, you know that, right? And if there's one thing Matthew Michael Holt isn't, it's stupid. Except whenever you're around 'Fluffy,'" she said, referring to Melissa by the less-than-flattering nickname she'd given the woman. "Then you have the brainpower of an amoeba on drugs.

"Matt, come out, come out wherever you—"

That was when she saw him.

And that was when she stifled the scream that rose up to her throat, a scream that came from Charley, Matt's sister, not Charley Randolph, police detective.

Stunned, frightened and in a complete daze, she dropped to her knees beside the body.

This was a dream, a nightmare, right? This wasn't happening. It wasn't!

"Matt, Matt, what has she done to you? Matt, *talk to me,*" she pleaded even as she felt his throat for his pulse.

And found none.

Somewhere in her horror-stricken haze, Charley managed to pull out her cell phone and press a key that was preset and quickly connected her to the necessary emergency number.

Her voice trembled as she spoke. "This is Detective Charlotte Randolph." She rattled off her badge number. "I need a bus. Officer down, I repeat, officer down. At 4832 Wayne Avenue. *Hurry,*" she begged.

She'd requested an ambulance rather than the coroner's wagon because maybe she was too numb to find the pulse, maybe he was still alive, his pulse reduced to a reedy whisper of a beat, hardly detectable at all.

The pulse Charley was praying that she had somehow missed.

Detective First Class Declan Cavanaugh turned in his swivel chair as he both listened to and watched his about-to-be-ex-partner Hollis Spenser give him the big news. Two years his senior, Hollis was leaving. Leaving the partnership, the department, the force. Leaving Aurora, California, for greener pastures.

"You're kidding."

Hollis moved the thatch of blond hair out of his eyes. "Nope. My new father-in-law thinks his daughter deserves a husband who comes home at night still breathing."

Cavanaugh frowned, regarding the man. "You look like you're breathing to me."

"You know what I mean." Hollis futilely pushed the hair out of his eyes, subconsciously knowing it would be back to position one in seconds. "Detectives who work in the private sector don't get shot at."

"Usually," Declan corrected. They all knew exceptions to *that* rule.

"Better odds," his partner of the past fifteen months corrected his almost-ex-partner's correction. Some habits died hard.

"Boring odds," Declan allowed. He shook his head as if he really pitied the man—and, in a way, he did. Hollis had just agreed to go willingly to serve a life sentence—unless this was his trade-off, what he intended to do until something better struck his fancy.

Still, Declan didn't back off right away. "You're going to be doing what, taking photographs of cheating husbands cheating on their wives, wives cheating on their husbands? Is that *really* what you want to be doing with your life ten years from now? *Trying* to do with your life?" he amended in case the battle wasn't going to be won with just one major skirmish.

"The pay's a lot better," Hollis confided with a triumphant air. "I'm going to be earning at least three times as much as what I get here. And no more 2:00 a.m. calls. I can sleep in."

"You sleep in half the time now," Declan pointed out to the man, his expression completely deadpan.

Hollis snorted as he went on packing up his desk. Eighteen months amounted to three boxes—full to capacity. "You're just jealous."

"Hey, you've got a pretty girl there, no doubt about it," he acknowledged, referring to his partner's new wife—everyone in the department had been invited to the reception and he had seen the woman up close and personal—or as personal as an ice cube could get. "But if *regular hours* means I've got to get married first, then you're welcome to regular hours.

"As for me, I'm never settling down just to constantly keep finding the same warm body next to me in bed morning in, morning out. I'm just not made that way. Can't think of anything worse," he admitted, adding in a shiver to underscore his feelings.

"Suit yourself," Hollis told him with a shrug. "But loving the same woman for the rest of your life, it has a lot going for it. I should know."

Yeah, Declan thought, he should. But it was obvious that his ex-partner didn't. He'd been brainwashed by a pro, if he knew his women.

"Enjoy it for both of us," he said philosophically, then sighed. "I guess this means that I've got to break in a new partner—again."

Hollis grinned. The look didn't suit him. It made him appear a little goofy, as if his energy was just flowing away. "Operative word here being *break?*"

"Hey, if they're not tough, they've got no business being a detective in Major Crimes," Declan pointed out. He had no patience with weakness of any kind and a police officer displaying those traits was worse than useless, no matter how charming this partner could be on his own.

"Yeah. Well, go easy on whoever the new partner they send up is. The department's only got so many detectives to go around." Hollis put his hand out to Declan. "It's been an experience, Declan. Keep in touch—and let me know if you ever want to start keeping regular hours. I'm sure the old man can find something for someone like you."

Declan supposed that was meant to flatter him.

It failed, through no fault of his well-intentioned about-to-be-ex-partner. "Not me. I like things to be unstructured," Declan told him. "Listen, I'll buy you a drink after hours—provided something else doesn't come up."

Hollis nodded. "You're on."

The acting lieutenant for Major Crimes stuck his head into Declan's tiny cubicle. "Hey, Cavanaugh, we got a call just now. Some officer got shot inside his own house."

"Domestic dispute?" Declan asked, saying the first thing that came to mind. He was already reaching into the drawer for the weapon he'd placed there.

"No details yet, just that another one of our detectives went to check on him and found the body in the living room. Check it out. And when you come back, come see me. We've got to look into getting you a new partner now that this one's making a break for it." He jerked a thumb in Hollis's direction.

"Just making plans to live the good life, Lieu, just making plans to live the good life," Hollis told his superior innocently.

"Yeah, well, come tell me that in six months," the lieutenant said. He stopped listening to the exchange between the two men the moment he turned away from them and headed back to his office.

"Looks like he's not going to be throwing you any farewell parties," Declan quipped. "Guess it's all up to me—if I can find anyone who knows who the hell you are," he added with a laugh.

Hollis could only shake his head. But he knew his limitations. Knew, too, that he might have very well invited a viper into his home space. With this in mind, he shook his head and proclaimed, "Nice, Cavanaugh, real nice."

Declan spread his hands wide, accentuating his innocent shrugs. "Hey, I just tell it the way I see it, man."

"Give my condolences to your new partner," Hollis called after him.

Declan nodded, then stopped short of the doorway and made a prediction as he shrugged into his jacket. "You'll be back."

"Keep telling yourself that, Cavanaugh," he chuckled, heading in the opposite direction. "You'll get old, waiting."

Declan shook his head. Had to be some kind of an epidemic, he decided. Some kind of a bug that was inducing people he knew—including his own siblings—to abandon their single existence, an existence that was highlighted by freedom and a myriad of choices in all directions—just to be yoked to another person, presumably for life.

And while he had to admit that he really liked and got along with the people that his brothers and sisters chose to become their "other halves," the

very hint of marriage, at least in his case, sounded
far too much like a prison sentence, he thought.

And that was definitely not for him.

Chapter 2

The sound of raised voices greeted Declan the minute he got out of his car, thanks to the wide-open door leading into the victim's house. Someone was having an argument, he thought, listening closely as he made his way up the walk.

"Look, Detective, there's no pulse," the paramedic with the two days' growth on his face argued. He gestured in exasperation toward the body on the sofa. "The officer's dead. There's nothing we can do for him. You've already made us apply the paddles once. There is no jump-starting this guy," he enunciated. "He's gone. You don't need an ambulance for him, you need the coroner's wagon. He's *dead*."

Declan looked from the two frustrated paramedics to the woman they were arguing with. The woman who, with her back to the entrance, was deliberately blocking the paramedics' exit.

"Try the paddles again," she ordered.

There was something vaguely familiar about the voice and the woman's stance, even though she had her back to him. Declan had the feeling that he knew her or, at the very least, that their paths had crossed once.

"He's gone, Detective," the other, older paramedic insisted, although his voice was gentler, more understanding than his partner's.

The woman rested her hand on the hilt of the weapon holstered at her side. The inference was difficult to miss.

"Just one more time," she told them evenly. "You can't be in *that* much of a hurry to leave."

The two paramedics exchanged looks, and then the younger one saw him standing in the doorway behind the detective. A silent appeal went out to Declan.

Declan inclined his head as if to say, "Humor her." The hope was that she would be easier to deal with if she was humored.

With a sigh, the taller of the two paramedics took out the defibrillator again, set it up to three hundred and held the flat surfaces out so that his partner could apply gel to the paddles. The first paramedic waited for thirty seconds, then cried out, "Clear!" just before applying the paddles to Matt's chest.

The officer's lifeless body jolted macabrely, rising an inch or so from the sofa, then fell back again, as devoid of any spark of life now as he had been the first time the paddles had been applied.

Still holding the paddles, the paramedic looked at her. "See?" he asked.

"Satisfied?" the other paramedic asked, more than ready to wrap things up and be on his way.

Charley closed her eyes, struggling to keep the hot tears back. She wasn't going to cry over Matt until she was alone, away from any prying eyes. She owed her brother that much, to conduct herself with dignity in public. Matt hated scenes.

"No," she said in what amounted to a strangled whisper. She wasn't satisfied at all. "But you can go."

The voice finally registered, setting off a chain reaction in Declan's head. He knew who she was now.

"Charlotte?" Declan asked, coming around to look at the detective's face. "Charlotte Randolph?" he asked for good measure, although he was fairly certain that he'd guessed correctly, identifying the powerhouse of a detective as the rookie he'd met while attending the academy. She'd been a go-getter back then, too—and married as he recalled. She was the one unattainable goddess all the male rookies fantasized about.

Charley looked up, climbing out of the temporary mental haze she'd descended into as the two paramedics made their way out of her brother's house, pushing the empty gurney before them. It took her a second to clear the fog from her brain.

Once she did, she immediately recognized the man who'd said her name. Declan Cavelli. Tall, gorgeous, broad-shouldered, slim-hipped Declan Cavelli. Best-looking would-be rookie cop at the academy. She vividly remembered wondering what it would have felt like, slipping her fingers through his thick, midnight-black hair, touching the silky straight strands. There probably wasn't a woman who crossed his path who didn't have fantasies about the man. And she was no exception.

Because routine was all she had now, she nodded her acknowledgment of his presence. "Cavelli."

Declan grinned. Thanks to his father, Sean, Declan and his siblings had discovered that due to a mix-up at the hospital where his father was born, they were actually Cavanaughs and not Cavellis as they had previously thought. It took some getting used to, but he was fine with it now. They all were.

"It's Cavanaugh now."

"You get married?" she deadpanned, doing her best to divorce herself from the very real body that was still on the sofa, waiting for proper documentation before the final fateful pickup conducted by the coroner's office.

"Long story," Declan quipped. "I'll tell you sometime—over drinks," he added. "Unless that jealous husband of yours still objects."

Even as he said it, he looked down at Charley's left hand. He was surprised to discover that it was as devoid of any jewelry as her right.

Did that mean she was divorced, or just trying to preserve her wedding ring?

Charley saw where the detective was looking and knew what he had to be wondering. "Long story," she said, echoing his words back to him.

Except that her story wasn't long. It was non-existent.

She'd never been married to begin with, but the class of rookies she had attended the academy with were a particularly aggressive group with testosterone all but swirling to overflowing—and Declan had been the biggest offender, as she recalled. It was a great deal easier just saying she was married than coming up with excuses and perpetually fending off the class of would-be Romeos. She attended the academy to learn everything there was about police work. Going out with any one of a number of the rookies—especially Declan—would have only served to blur her focus.

So she opted to pretend she was already off the market and married. Only a handful had tried to change her mind about remaining faithful to her vows and they soon gave up when she showed no signs of coming around to their way of thinking.

"I like long stories," he told her. "We'll trade them." Then, turning his attention to the reason he'd been called out to begin with, he nodded at the dead man. He would have had to have been deaf and blind to miss the distress in her voice and on her face and he was neither. "He a friend of yours?"

"We knew each other," Charley answered, keeping her reply deliberately vague. If she admitted to Declan that Matt was her half brother, she knew that there wouldn't be a chance in hell she would be allowed to work on his murder. And right now that was the most important thing in the world to her.

Declan took her answer in stride. "How did you happen to be here?" he asked.

Charley looked up sharply, recognizing the tone Declan was using. It was deliberately laid-back, conversational—and moving in for the kill because, as the person who called in the murder, she was suspect number one.

She told him the truth—as far as she was willing to take it.

"I heard Holt hadn't shown up for his shift in the last couple of days and his lieutenant said he hadn't called in, either. That wasn't like Holt. I knew he was having a hard time because of a breakup he was going through, so I decided to stop by to check on him. It was on my way." It hadn't been, but Cavelli—or Cavanaugh—didn't need to know that part, Charley thought.

"A breakup?" Declan echoed, looking at her thoughtfully. "With you?"

The question was so unexpected, it made her laugh. The laugh was devoid of any humor.

"Hardly. Her name was Melissa. They didn't quite have the same goals and expectations. When Holt looked at her, he heard wedding bells ringing. When she looked at him, she heard the sound of a cash register going off."

"Not a match made in heaven," Declan agreed. He looked down at the man thoughtfully. "You think he killed himself?"

"He wasn't the type." He wouldn't have done that to her, no matter how badly he'd been hurting. He wouldn't have taken himself out of her life like that.

"Then you knew him pretty well," Declan concluded.

She didn't want Declan to go veering onto that path, but rather than deny it, she gave him another answer. "There was a note," she began.

Declan eyed her, his interest escalated. "A suicide note?"

"No," Charley snapped, the edge of her temper growing frayed at an increasingly faster pace. She knew she wasn't being fair to Declan. It wasn't his fault that Matt was dead.

It bothered her greatly that there were no defensive wounds on the body. That meant that Matt hadn't fought back. Most likely, he'd been passed out when the killer had struck.

She hadn't had time to do anything with the note except carefully remove it so that it wouldn't get damaged when the paramedics worked over her brother. Taking her handkerchief out, she picked up the edge of the paper she'd placed out of the way and held it up for Declan to read.

"Just the beginning," Declan repeated, and raised his eyes to her face. "You think it's a budding serial killer making an announcement?"

"Could be," she allowed, then told him the last detail. "It was stapled to his chest."

That didn't sound right. Was she getting muddled because the discovery of the body had hit her hard? "You mean to his shirt."

"No," she said, taking out her cell phone and selecting the photos app. "To his chest."

She flipped through the photographs to the one she'd made herself take of Matt, knowing it was an important detail that just might help them solve Matt's murder.

Finding the one she was looking for, she held it up for Declan. "There. See?"

"Wow." The word just slipped out of its own volition. He took the smart phone from her—or tried to. "I won't damage it," he promised her.

She was really going to have to get a better grip on herself or she wasn't going to be of any use to Matt, she upbraided herself.

"Sorry," Charley responded, releasing her hold on the phone.

"That's okay," Declan said. And then he took a closer look at the photograph that she had queued up for his perusal. "You're right, the note *was* stapled to his chest. Who does that kind of thing?" he marveled, more to himself than to her.

That was an easy one to answer. It was all the other questions that were going to be difficult. "Someone who's crazy."

"Any more? Photos?" he asked rather than just arbitrarily flip through her array of photographs. In what he saw as her present, rather fragile state, he wanted to make sure he avoided doing anything that might upset her any further than she already was.

"Not of the crime scene," she told him. There were other photographs of Matt, both with her and without her, but those she didn't want this detective to see. If the matter came up, she wouldn't deny her connection to Matt, but until then, she wasn't about to advertise the fact that he was her brother, either.

Declan leaned over the officer's body, taking in all he could without actually touching the man or rolling him over. The bullet seemed to have entered in the region of his heart. He had no way of knowing if there was an exit wound until after the crime-scene investigator released the body. He wondered if his father had been called in for this one. Seeing as how it was a police officer who had been shot—possibly executed—he rather thought it was likely that his father would be on the scene since he was head of the day lab unit.

"Think he means it?" Declan asked, straightening up again.

The detective had asked the question completely out of the blue. She stared at him, unclear what he was referring to. "Who?"

"The killer," Declan told her patiently. "Do you think there'll be more? That he really intends to kill other people?"

Charley shrugged, at a loss to form any real opinion. "That's what his note says," she replied, her voice eerily removed.

Declan nodded as he conducted a perimeter examination of the area where the body had been discovered. "Well, thanks for the input," he told her. "I'll keep you in the loop if I can."

Charley didn't budge as she gave him a glare that would have made Medusa shiver. "'In the loop'?" she echoed incredulously. "I'm not going to be in any 'loop,' Cavelli or Cavanaugh or whatever name you want to go by," she informed him. "I'm going to work this case."

"What department are you with?" he asked her patiently.

She knew where he was going with this. "Narcotics. It doesn't matter," Charley insisted, immediately vetoing any objections he might have been inclined to raise. "I was the first on the scene and I'm..." she paused to search for just the right words to use in this argument she intended to win "...familiar with his...with the victim's background. That is definitely going to prove handy."

"This is a homicide," Declan began.

There were a variety of reasons why she couldn't work the case, objections he was rather certain his lieutenant would raise—unless Declan went to bat for her. He rolled the thought over in his head. He was officially minus a partner and this was not a one-man investigation—especially if it turned out that this killer had more bodies on his agenda.

Thinking it over, he decided that that would most likely prove to be the best argument to use when he spoke to his lieutenant.

"I *know* what it is," Charley retorted, grinding out the words. "Look, I need to be included in this investigation—actively included," she underscored before he found some cute little phrase to insultingly refer to her participation in this investigation.

She took a breath, knowing what she was about to do was going to make her vulnerable, but she had no option left to her. She owed it to Matt to find his killer—to avenge his death. "Look, I'll be in your debt if you talk to your captain—"

"Lieutenant," Declan corrected.

"Whatever." Charley shrugged impatiently. Her eyes held his, waiting for a decision from him.

"In my debt," Declan repeated thoughtfully. He *did* like the sound of that.

"In your debt," she confirmed, her voice as devoid of emotion as she could make it. Later she'd figure out how to get around this deal with the devil she was making, but right now, she had to secure her position on the investigation.

"You want in that badly?" Declan asked, scrutinizing her closely. There were things she wasn't telling him, but he was rather certain they would surface, by and by.

She raised her chin like a soldier about to charge into the unknown and, just possibly, not return again. "Yes."

"Okay," he agreed. "I'll talk to my lieutenant, see if he can get you temporarily assigned to Major Crimes. You just might be in luck. My partner handed in his papers today and he's leaving the department for the private sector."

Charley nodded, but she hardly heard a word of what the other detective was saying to her. The phrase "you just might be in luck" was echoing over and over again in her head.

She was never going to be in luck again.

Her brother, her best friend, her *entire family* lay on the sofa, dead.

There was no such thing as luck anymore, she thought darkly.

She didn't realize Cavanaugh was talking to her, didn't even hear him, let alone have any of his words register until she felt someone touch her arm. Blinking she looked up, once again abandoning the haze she hadn't even realized she'd slipped back into.

"Are you all right?" Declan was asking.

She roused herself, doing her best to look alert and generally unfazed. She had her suspicions she couldn't quite carry off the impression that she'd come around. "Why shouldn't I be?"

Declan began to enumerate the reasons that occurred to him. "Well, for one thing, you look like you're a million miles away."

Charley shrugged. She had that one covered. "That's not exactly a pretty sight to emboss on my brain," she replied flippantly, indicating the dead body on the sofa.

There was more going on here than that and Declan knew it. Moreover, he was fairly certain that she knew he knew it. But now wasn't the time to get into it. He had to give her a little time to collect herself—while he did a little digging on the side into her background.

Keeping her close would turn out to be a good thing, Declan decided. Other than the fact that— strictly speaking as a man—she was even more of a knockout now than she had been back in the academy, she was obviously mixed up in this some-how. Whether merely innocently because she was acquainted with the victim or if there was more to it than that, he'd yet to decide, but she figured into all this somehow and he intended to use that to his advantage.

He was fairly confident he could sell this to the lieutenant. The man trusted his judgment and more important than that, he wanted to stay on the good side of the chief of detectives, Brian Cavanaugh, and Brian took a personal interest in all his detec-tives, especially those bearing the same surname as his.

All that remained for him to figure out, once the dust settled and he—or they—found the killer, was what he intended to get in exchange for letting her come on board and work with him.

This was going to be very interesting, he decided as he heard the sound of what he presumed was the crime-scene investigative unit's vehicle approaching.

Chapter 3

Sean Cavanaugh was the first crime-scene investigator in through the doorway.

Nodding at his son and the unfamiliar woman with him—was it him, or did it seem like there was *always* a woman with Declan?—the head of the day investigative unit looked grimly down at the body on the sofa. The dead man appeared to be in his late twenties, early thirties. Strong, well built and undoubtedly with a good future in front of him until a bullet ended all that.

What a waste, Sean thought, setting down the case he always carefully checked and restocked after every crime-scene investigation. It was time to get to work and find answers.

"So the victim's one of our own," Sean said sadly, addressing the remark to both of the occupants within the room.

Charley answered first. "Yes, sir, he was. Sergeant Matthew Holt," she told the head of CSI.

Oh, Matt, Matt, what have you gone and let happen to you? Why'd you let your guard down like that? You always told me to be careful. Why weren't you?

Charley felt her throat closing, suddenly clogged with tears. She fought them back.

Sean nodded, taking in the information. "And you are?" he asked.

"Detective Charlotte Randolph, sir." Charley focused strictly on answering the questions put to her. Her voice sounded almost robotlike. "I was the one who called it in."

Sean unlocked his case and lifted the lid. "Well, Charlotte—"

"Charley," she corrected him, forcing a faint smile to her lips. "People call me Charley."

Matt had called her Charley when she was a little girl and the name had stuck, she thought now. Damn it, she couldn't tear up, she couldn't, Charley ordered herself, digging her nails into her palms.

Think of something else. Think of anything else.

Sean looked at the woman, quietly studying her. This wasn't just a casual acquaintance of the victim. His death was affecting her.

"Well, Charley," Sean amended. "How did you happen to be here?" he asked gently.

"I already asked her that," Declan interjected.

"Yes, but I didn't," his father pointed out calmly. Both his voice and his expression were sympathetic as he continued to regard the young woman.

Behind him, two more members of his investigative team came in, both well entrenched in what their particular duties were at a scene like this. They got to work quickly and quietly, moving as smoothly as the timing belt on a well-oiled engine.

Charley took a breath before reciting her answer. "I heard he hadn't shown up for work for a couple of days and that he hadn't even bothered calling in. I knew that wasn't like him, but I also knew that he was going through a rough patch—"

"What kind of a rough patch?" Sean asked.

"He'd just broken up with a woman he was certain was 'the one.'" Someone should have strangled Melissa a long time ago, she thought angrily. Before the witch ever came into Matt's life.

Guided by her tone, Sean made the only logical assumption. "But she wasn't 'the one,' was she?"

"Not unless we were talking about barracudas, sir," Charley replied, deliberately staring straight ahead, past the CSI chief's head.

"No need to call me sir," Sean said. That sort of thing created a formal atmosphere and right now, he was striving for the exact opposite. Nodding his head to indicate Declan, he added, "He never does."

"I do, too. You just don't listen," Declan told his father.

"All too well, Declan," Sean said, glancing at his son knowingly. "All too well. All right, if you two want to stand over there and wait until I finish processing the crime scene, it shouldn't be all that long." He glanced at the opened bottles of vodka and Kahlua on the coffee table. "A little early in the day to be getting into that right now. Was that his drink of choice?" he asked. "A black Russian?"

It hadn't been, initially. All Matt ever drank— if he drank at all—was a beer, maybe on rare occasions, two. He hadn't been very big on anything that allowed him to lose the tight rein he had over his control.

"It was a habit he picked up from Melissa," Charley told him.

Declan scanned the room as if that could somehow answer his questions by the very nature of the vibrations that had been left behind. "Then maybe she was here, too," he suggested.

"Only one glass," Charley pointed out. "It was the first thing I checked for." Once she could bring herself to leave Matt where he lay, she added silently. "Besides, there's no lipstick on the glass."

"Big on makeup, was she?" Declan asked, curious. This detective seemed to know a lot about the woman in question. Why?

"It helped to cover up her physical flaws," she explained.

He laughed at the way she worded her answer. "Not a big fan of the woman in question, I take it."

Charley saw no reason to deny or cover up how she felt about the woman who had deliberately broken her brother's heart. What did it matter? Matt was gone and his feelings were the only ones that had ever mattered to her anyway. If she'd held her tongue before about Melissa, it was only to spare him.

In hindsight, maybe if she had said something, he wouldn't have gotten to this point. Maybe he might have even been alive now because he would have been at work, not home and unprotected.

"I wouldn't lift a finger to save her if she was drowning in a puddle of rainwater," Charley told the detective.

"Talk about cold," Declan couldn't help commenting.

Actually, it was the exact opposite. Whenever she thought of the strawberry-blonde with the flat brown eyes who had led her brother around as if he were some sort of trained monkey on a leash, her blood pressure went up by at least ten points. Possibly even more.

"She cut out his heart and stomped on it. I have

no reason to get all warm and toasty whenever I think of her—which is as infrequently as possible," she informed Declan, her tone indicating that she didn't want to discuss the woman anymore.

"Duly noted," Sean said. For a minute, she'd forgotten the other man was still in the room.

The head of CSI took out the camera he'd paid for with his own money, preferring to use something he was comfortable with rather than the one the department had issued to him.

"Will you two be working the case together?" he asked mildly.

Declan said, "Don't know yet" at the same time that Charley said, "Yes."

Sean smiled. "A slight difference of opinion, I see. Apparently the situation is all tangled up, which is nothing new." He lowered the camera for a moment to look at her. "I'll keep Declan here posted and he can let you know what progress has been made, if any."

She didn't want to be on the receiving end of anything secondhand. "If it's all the same to you, I'd like to stop by the lab whenever you're done processing the evidence."

Sean glanced up for a moment, assessing the woman in front of him. Seeing the expression in her eyes. There was that pain again, he noted. Definite pain. This wasn't just a fellow brother in blue she'd looked in on. This was someone important to her.

For now, he let it go at that. He had a crime scene to process. "Give me your card, Charley." She was quick to oblige him, digging out one of the cards the department had issued to her.

Matt had his own made up for her at the same time. The cards were identical—except for the drawing of a teddy bear on the front. The image represented Barney the Bear, another toy he'd given her. One, he told her, that was supposed to keep her company and protect her whenever she felt afraid.

Barney was propped up on her bed where, even now, he spent his days and nights, a vivid connection to her childhood.

And now he would also serve as a reminder of the brother she'd lost today, she couldn't help thinking.

Steady, Charley warned herself.

Sean tucked the card into his pocket and went on taking photographs of the crime scene.

"Your friend have any enemies?" Declan asked as they walked out of the house.

She hated leaving Matt there, lifeless on the sofa, no longer regarded as a person, just a statistic. But she knew she had to. There was nothing she could do for him now—except find his killer.

"None," she answered the detective.

"How about this ex-girlfriend?" he prodded. "Melissa?"

Charley shook her head. As much as she hated

the woman, she knew Melissa wasn't responsible for Matt's murder. "Melissa didn't do this."

Declan looked at her with more than mild interest. "What makes you so sure?"

"To begin with, she's not bright enough to know how to work a stapler," Charley said sarcastically, referring to the note that had been stapled to Matt's chest. "And the note said this was only the beginning. That means whoever did it was holding Matt accountable for something and he—or she—was obviously holding other people accountable, as well."

"Accountable for what?" Declan asked.

Charley shook her head in complete frustration. "I don't know."

For now, he took her at her word. "Fair enough. But there's also another explanation, you know."

She looked at him, waiting. She certainly couldn't think of any. "Which is?"

"Maybe whoever did it wanted to make it sound as if there were going to be other fatalities to throw us off. Maybe Holt was the killer's only intended victim."

The theory had merit, she supposed. "It's a possibility," Charley allowed, even though she didn't want to. This gave them far too many possibilities, far too many avenues to investigate.

Well, at least he got her to admit that, Declan thought. Maybe this meant she wasn't as terminally stubborn as she used to be. "This Melissa, you know her last name?"

"Merryweather," Charley told him, then repeated, "She didn't do it."

Declan nodded, barely paying attention to her. He was busy forming plans in his head.

"So you said. Humor me." And then he realized that she could still be of some more use. "You wouldn't by any chance know where we could find her, would you?"

Charley's expression was totally unreadable. "Other than under the first rock you come to, no."

"That's okay, I can look her up once I get back to the office."

He didn't ask her if she wanted a ride, because she had her own vehicle as far as he knew and besides, he was really hoping she'd given up the idea of working this with him. As gorgeous as the woman was, he had a feeling that working with her might be a challenge he'd save for another day.

Pulling out of the driveway, he left the other detective standing there, watching him take off.

Declan didn't think about her again until he was pulling up in the police department's rear parking lot. The woman he'd left behind him was now standing by the rear entrance into the building.

Stunned, he slammed the driver's door behind him as he jumped out of his vehicle. He cut the distance to her in long, quick strides, hardly remembering making them.

"How the hell did you get here ahead of me?" he asked.

That was probably the easiest question she was going to field this week. She gave him a quick, pasted-on smile. "I drive faster than you do. You drive like a senior citizen," she pointed out. "Let's go up to talk to your lieutenant," she said, reminding him of his promise.

"Might as well," he said, resigned as he punched the number 3 on the keypad on the silver wall. "And I drive carefully," he corrected, taking offense at her assessment.

"Whatever you say," she replied.

When they got to the office, Lieutenant Jacobs was nowhere to be found.

"Personal emergency," one of the other detectives in the department told them when Declan came out of the man's office. "His wife lost control of her car—it wound up as window dressing in a boutique showroom. The lieutenant looked fit to be tied once he knew for certain his wife hadn't killed herself. My guess is that he won't be back today. You need help with something?" the man asked, giving Charley a scrutinizing once-over.

"No," Declan answered. Turning toward the woman with him, he said, "Looks like I'm on my own here."

"We're on our own." She deliberately emphasized the first word.

"Hey, Cavanaugh, wanna introduce me?" the detective he'd just been talking to asked, rising to his feet as he was taught in a bygone wonderfully polite era.

"No," Declan replied succinctly as he walked away, headed to his desk. "Okay, let me see if I can find this Melissa Merryweather," he said more to himself than to Charley.

He just didn't give up, did he? she thought. Well, it was his time he was wasting. But she intended to try to follow up any shred of a lead the CSI people came up with.

"You're barking up the wrong tree," she told him mildly.

He was getting tired of hearing her say that. "Well, unless and until another tree comes leaping out at me, this is all I've—we've—" he corrected himself before she could "—got. Unless you're keeping something from me," he tagged on.

She was, but it had nothing to do with Matt's murder and everything to do with her being able to investigate it, so she kept the information to herself as she shook her head. "Not a thing."

In his opinion, Charley sounded entirely too innocent when she said that and he always held displays of innocence to that degree suspect. But he had nothing to go on other than a gut instinct, one he wasn't able to pin down or flesh out yet. Until such time, he intended to keep this detective close to him and the best way to do that was to allow her to think he was all for their joining forces.

Getting comfortable at his desk, he gestured to the somewhat scarred desk facing his.

"Spenser was moving out his stuff when I left here this morning. Looks like he's finished so you can park yourself there for the time being if you like."

She pulled the chair out and sank down into it. It was going to need some adjustment. This Spenser was a big man, she concluded. "Spenser your partner?"

"Ex-partner." Declan didn't look up, his fingers gliding along the keyboard as he continued to search for Melissa Merryweather's address. "He decided he could make more money in the private sector."

That wasn't exactly a newsworthy discovery. "He probably can," she speculated. The police department wasn't exactly known for its princely salaries. "You two work together long?"

He had to think for a moment before answering. "A little over a year and a half."

"Get along?"

That caught his attention. "Average," he acknowledged, looking at her sharply. "What's with the twenty questions?" he asked. What was she up to? Even back in the academy, he remembered that Charley had an agenda, a schedule. She went at training doggedly—a preview of how she handled everything else. He doubted that a leopard could change its spots.

"Just catching up," she said. Moreover, if Declan was answering questions, he couldn't be asking them.

"That works two ways," he reminded her. "I get a chance to catch up, too." He had a few outstanding questions about her he wanted to ask—especially about that mysterious husband of hers who had devolved into a long story for a slow night.

Rather than comment on what he'd just pointed out, Charley indicated the computer he was typing on. "Find anything yet?"

No, and it wasn't for lack of trying, he thought in frustration.

"Program's slow," he said out loud. "The department's way overdue in investing in new computers to keep us up to speed." The fact that his department wasn't alone in this didn't make it any more palatable for him. Declan had never ascribed to the "misery loves company" way of thinking.

"Could be worse," Charley offered philosophically.

He frowned at the blank screen with its maddening note at the bottom that told him it was "waiting to connect."

"How?"

"You could still be banging out end-of-day re-ports on typewriters and have to make do with just one computer to a floor."

Now she was just making things up, he thought. "*Nobody's* that archaic."

"Oh, you'd be surprised," she countered.

The last police department she'd considered ap-plying to, located in a little town in New Mexico, had a force of exactly three—a sheriff and two dep-uties—for the entire county, and the only accessible computer was located in the town's one-story public library. The deputies and the sheriff's secretary did all their work on electric typewriters.

"You'll have to tell me about it someday," he told her in a voice that indicated "someday" wasn't going to be anytime soon. A second later, he trium-phantly announced, "Got her."

Charley didn't have to ask who.

Chapter 4

Melissa Merryweather tended bar in a cocktail lounge within one of Aurora's more upscale hotels. The Aurora Maxwell was located on a major thoroughfare and was approximately a mile away from the city's commuter airport.

Given the hour, the lounge was close to empty with only a couple of harried travelers seated at tables for one, looking to unwind.

The ambience—semidarkness—was either soothing or depressing, depending on the point of view of the person taking it in. Charley found it depressing. The thought of sitting on a stool at the bar, ruminating over a half-filled glass of alcohol only made it more so.

The less-than-genuine smile on Melissa's carefully made-up face widened as she looked up when Declan walked into the lounge. It was obvious to Charley that although both of them were approaching the bar at an equal pace, Melissa only saw him.

It was like watching a predator come to life, Charley thought. Even Melissa's strawberry-blond, corkscrew curls seemed to become bouncier.

"Hi, handsome, what can I get you?" Melissa asked in a husky voice that Charley thought was probably more suitable for someone making an obscene phone call, which she wouldn't have put past Melissa.

"A few answers," Declan replied, the width of his smile matching hers.

Except on him, Charley had to admit, the smile looked rather seductive—make that *very* seductive. It was obvious that Melissa was aware of it.

"How about we start with 'yes'?" Melissa suggested, leaning in as close as she could to him, given that there was a bar between them. It didn't take a rocket scientist to see that she was flirting with him for all she was worth and it was only partially to get him to spend money at the bar.

In her mind, Melissa was probably already going home with him.

This was the woman who had gotten her hooks into her brother, who had taken him for everything she could, then tossed him aside, filleted and aching. For two cents, Charley would have loved to sink her fist into that annoying face.

It was a struggle to hold her tongue and not tell the woman to drop the act and behave like a responsible person. For all she knew, to Melissa, this *was* her idea of a responsible person. The woman had the IQ of a dirty shoelace.

Declan appeared unmoved by the woman's blatant flirtation, although he remained friendly. "How about, where were you last night?"

Melissa shrugged dismissively, as if that was of no consequence. "No place special. But I can be anywhere you want me to be tonight."

Okay, enough was enough. Any more of this and she was going to be nauseous.

"We need you to be more specific than 'no place special,'" Charley interjected.

The pretty forehead furrowed and a look of annoyance crossed her face as she regarded her. "Why?"

"It's not your turn to ask questions yet," Charley informed her curtly.

The furrowed brow became more so as Melissa stared at her. "Don't I know you from someplace?" she asked, struggling to remember.

"That's another question," Charley pointed out, determined not to give Melissa a scrap of information.

Anger etched a line into her features. "Listen, you—"

"That's 'Detective' You," Charley corrected wryly. "And we still need to know where you were last night—and early this morning," she added since her brother's time of death hadn't been established yet.

"You're police?" Melissa asked, the last of the friendliness evaporating from her voice.

Declan had taken a backseat for a moment, amused at the exchange between the two women. He had a feeling that Charley had it in her to be a real spitfire if she wanted to be.

But since the woman behind the bar had asked a legitimate question, he decided maybe he should step up before the situation really spun out of control.

"Afraid so," he told her, taking out his identification for her viewing. "Detectives Cavanaugh and Randolph," he said, introducing himself to her.

"Terrific," Melissa muttered. The brightness had definitely left her smile. "Did Matt send you to hassle me?" she demanded.

"Why would he do that?" Declan asked, his voice marginally interested.

"Because I broke up with the loser," she snapped, rubbing at a spot on the bar that wouldn't give up its stain. "It's not my fault he thought it was serious between us."

"Right. He should have realized that the only serious affair you could have was with money," Charley murmured under her breath.

She knew better, and ordinarily she would have refrained from saying something like that, but she wasn't exactly thinking clearly at the moment and her temper had gotten away from her.

"You can't talk to me like that!" Melissa cried indignantly.

"Actually, she could probably talk a lot worse to you than that, so I wouldn't push it if I were you," Declan warned her, completely surprising Charley. Whether he realized it or not, he'd just helped her regain control over her temper.

All Melissa seemed to be aware of was being insulted. "Look, you give Matt a message for me. You tell him I don't care who he sends over, we're not getting back together and that's final."

Declan inclined his head. "I'm afraid it is."

The bartender looked somewhat perplexed. For the moment, her confusion paralyzed her. "You mean you think he'll back off?"

"Sergeant Holt can't do very much of anything anymore," Declan informed her. "He's dead."

The woman behind the bar appeared stunned, as if the person she'd just been talking to had lapsed into a language she couldn't comprehend. "What?" she asked hoarsely, staring at Declan.

"He's dead," Charley repeated, struggling to

keep her voice from cracking. Her eyes darted to Declan to see if he noticed her momentary shift in tone, but he seemed only focused on Melissa.

Was that because he still thought of the woman as a suspect, or because the vest Melissa was wearing set off her breasts to their best advantage, emphasizing her cleavage?

Charley couldn't decide.

"This is a joke, right?" Melissa asked, glancing at her and then Declan, waiting for one of them to tell her she was right.

Charley took out her phone and showed her the photo she'd taken of her brother at the crime scene, the cryptic note still pinned to his chest. "This isn't a joke," she said.

Melissa stared wide-eyed at the picture on the cell phone, then turned her head away. "Oh, God, he's dead in that, isn't he?" she asked, directing the question to Declan. Upset or not, she never lost her focus, which meant playing to the best-looking man in the room.

"Yes, he is," Declan replied patiently, knowing that if he left it to Charley to answer her, he couldn't be sure just what would come out.

Anyone paying minimal attention could see that she didn't like the woman. Was that because she felt Melissa had treated Holt badly—or because she was jealous of the connection, however brief, the two had had?

"How did it happen?" Melissa asked. "Was it the bullet that killed him?" Her eyes strayed back to the photograph and the hole in Matt's chest.

"Well, it didn't help," Charley snapped.

Then, to her surprise, she saw tears shining in the other woman's eyes. Given what she knew about their relationship, she wouldn't have thought Melissa capable of any genuine grief or any real emotion whatsoever. There was a chance that she had misjudged the woman—but she tended not to believe that.

"I'm sorry," Melissa said. "I've got to go sit down somewhere."

Coming around the bar, rather than take a seat the way she'd indicated, Melissa went straight to Declan and leaned heavily against him, her chest heaving with supposedly trapped sobs.

Making eye contact with him, Charley didn't even try to hide her disdain. She rolled her eyes, letting him know exactly what she thought of this little performance.

"Who did it?" Melissa asked.

"That's what we're trying to find out," Declan replied, looking around for a likely place to deposit the woman who at this point was all over him. Under different circumstances, it might have even been a pleasant enough interlude, but given the situation, having her like this was rather awkward and uncomfortable.

Charley grabbed the back of a chair and unceremoniously shoved it against the back of Melissa's legs, causing them to buckle. The next moment, the bartender found herself landing in the chair with a thud. She swung her head around and glared accusingly at Charley, who in turn smiled innocently at her and reminded her, "You said you needed to sit down."

Melissa's glare vanished as she turned her brown eyes toward Declan.

"You can't think that I had anything to do with it," she protested, obviously feeling that was enough to terminate any further questions.

She was surprised then to hear Declan ask, "Did you?"

"No!" she exclaimed loudly. "We were finished and he finally got that through his thick skull. I didn't have to kill him," she declared flatly.

And then suddenly, just as the topic seemed to be closing, Melissa's eyes widened and she looked at Charley, recognition setting in. "You're his—his friend, aren't you?" she asked. "Don't deny it, I recognize you. There's a picture of you in his house."

"I have no intention of denying it," Charley told her coolly. "We were friends—and I want to find out what happened to my friend." There was just the slightest pause between the last two words, one she hoped Declan didn't hear. "And for what it's worth, I don't think you did it."

"Oh." Caught off guard, Melissa smiled, almost magnanimously. "You don't?"

"No, I don't," Charley replied. "Something like that takes a lot of planning. That's not exactly your strong point."

Brow furrowed again, Melissa looked at Declan. "Did she just insult me?"

"No," he reassured her. "From where I'm standing, she was just stating a fact."

"Oh," Melissa murmured, her expression that of a woman who was clearly bewildered.

What in heaven's name had her brother ever seen in this half-witted woman? Granted Melissa Merryweather's body was a knockout, but Matt had standards. He had a brain and he required conversation, at least occasionally. From all indications, Melissa had the kind of brain where thoughts went to die, not flourish, Charley thought.

And then she shrugged inwardly. She supposed that everyone had their weak point, their waterloo. Matt's reaction to Melissa didn't have to make sense to her, it only had to make it to him, she decided.

Melissa looked rather subdued as she asked Declan, "Do I really need an alibi for last night?"

"It would help," he told her.

Melissa sighed, as if she knew that what she was about to say took her out of any game that might be played out between her and the good-looking detective, at least for tonight.

"I was with Josh," she reluctantly told him.

"Josh?" Declan repeated, waiting for more.

Melissa shrugged, annoyed to be put in this sort of a spot. "I don't know his last name. He's staying here at the hotel for a few days. Business," she added importantly, then recited, "Room number 805. He stayed here until closing time last night and then we went up to his room."

"Unbelievable," Charley murmured under her breath.

She looked to Declan to wrap this preliminary—and hopefully the only—interview and do what they had to do to tie this up with a bow. She was anxious to begin actively investigating Matt's murder. This was only a waste of time.

Melissa's story checked out.

"Josh" in room 805 was Josh Walters and he confirmed that she had spent the night with him. The pharmaceutical sales rep was more than willing to volunteer a detailed account of their sleepless, active night together.

"That's all right," Charley said, cutting him short, "we just needed to have her alibi confirmed."

"It's confirmed all right," Josh said with bright-eyed enthusiasm. "I had no idea the human body could bend that way," he said with a laugh. And then he suddenly sobered. "Hey, she's not in any trouble, is she?"

"None except with her conscience," Charley said.

"'Cause I don't even know the woman," he continued as if nothing had been said in response.

"Other than the fact that she's very flexible," Declan interjected.

Josh had the good grace to look embarrassed. "Yeah, except for that."

The sales rep looked from one detective to the other. "Am I free to go? 'Cause I have this meeting I'm supposed to be attending at three—"

"You're as free as a bird," Declan told him. The hotel door instantly closed on both of them, the sales rep gladly putting both of them—and most likely his friendly bartender—into his past.

With a sigh, Declan headed for the elevator. "Well, you were right." Charley could see that it had taken a lot for him to admit that.

"About?" she asked quizzically.

Each word seemed to cost him. "That she didn't do it."

Charley nodded. She saw no reason to gloat. He was just doing what a good detective did and she was just going by her gut.

"Yeah, I know." There was no joy in being right this time. "I kind of wish she had."

Her response caught him off guard. "What? Why?"

"So we could stick her butt in jail. That would be

fitting payback. That kind of woman just spreads grief and misery wherever she goes."

"But flexibly," Declan deadpanned, still able to see the humor in the situation.

"Huh," Charley commented. "I wonder if that means you can tie her into a knot."

"Might be interesting to find out," Declan mused. He frowned just slightly, not remembering having parked this far from the hotel entrance.

Charley became serious as they approached his vehicle. She was still rather uneasy about her place in the investigation. This was his show and he actually had the right to keep her out of it—even if she had no intention of stepping aside.

So, in as respectful a voice as she could manage, she inquired, "Now what?"

Declan had to admit that he was surprised she was deferring to him. He would have bet money that, fired up, Charley would have tried to take over the investigation, forcing him to take a backseat to her even if she didn't belong on this case at all.

Was she pretending to defer to him in order to stay on his good side? After all, technically, she didn't really belong on this investigation to begin with.

Getting into the car, he waited until she was in on her side and buckled up.

"You know you can't work this case with me indefinitely, right?"

Well, that didn't take long. Charley felt as if he'd just prodded her with a hot poker.

"Why not?"

Did he really have to explain it to her? Or was she doing this to make him relent and let her continue working with him?

"Because you're from a different department and there are rules about this sort of thing," Declan pointed out. To be honest, he just assumed there were rules to follow since obviously detectives couldn't just work whatever case they wanted to. A lot of cases would go begging if that was true.

"Who can overrule the rules?" Charley asked.

Since Declan wasn't sure if his lieutenant was coming in tomorrow, that more or less left him in charge of himself, but he wasn't about to tell her that.

In settling the matter of jurisdiction over a case, aside from the head of his department, only one name came to mind.

"The chief of Ds," he told her.

"Good enough for me," Charley murmured, already working on her strategy to get the man to side with her.

To her way of thinking, it was the only smart, economical way to proceed. For one thing, officially or unofficially, she intended to work this case until it was solved. For another, she was going to use her downtime to see if there was an angle they missed going over. She'd think that the chief of detectives would have wanted his detectives working together, not haphazardly, when it came to working on the murder of one of their own.

She was prepared to tell him that once she was granted an audience with the man.

Chapter 5

The connection between his father and the chief of detectives had come out more than a year ago, but there were times, Declan admitted to himself, when he still found it odd and a touch surprising that he and his siblings were actually directly related to Brian Cavanaugh, the chief of detectives. The man who was in charge of them all.

Nodding at his secretary, a formidable woman who had seen her share of street action early in her career, Declan knocked on his uncle's door.

A deep voice from within the office said a single word, "Come."

Rather than walk in once he'd opened the door

to his uncle's office, Declan first stuck his head in and asked, "Got a minute?"

Brian Cavanaugh smiled, a hint of amusement highlighting his deep, deep blue eyes. He checked his watch.

"Three, actually. Come in, Declan," he invited. Seeing that his nephew wasn't alone, Brian half rose in his seat, inclining his head by way of a greeting.

Belatedly, Declan realized his omission and made the introduction—or at least began to. "Sorry," he apologized for the oversight. "This is—"

Brian's smile widened just a touch as he extended his hand to the young woman. "Detective Charley Randolph, yes, I know."

The greeting took Charley slightly aback as she shook the hand that was held out to her. Brian Cavanaugh's hand seemed to all but swallow hers up. Even so, the contact managed to create a feeling of well-being rather than a feeling of being lost within something that was larger than she.

"You do?" she asked. To her best recollection, she had never had any interaction with the chief of detectives before, other than seeing him at a distance.

Brian nodded as he gestured toward the two chairs on the other side of his desk. His meaning was clear. Declan and Charley took their seats.

"I make it a habit of being familiar with all the

detectives who work under me," Brian replied. "It makes for a more efficient police department."

Declan slid to the edge of his seat. He had no intention of overstaying. "Then you know that Lieutenant Jacobs had a family emergency that's taken him away from the department."

Brian nodded grimly. "Scares a man to death to hear that kind of news about his wife." He received a report regarding the accident within minutes of its occurrence. To his way of thinking, they were all part of one very large family unit. "But she came out of surgery well and the operating surgeon believes that she'll make a full recovery quickly."

How did he do it? Charley wondered. How did the man stay on top of things like that and still keep tabs on what went on within the different departments and the cases they were working on? Talk about multitasking. The man probably only got about three to five hours of sleep a night—if that.

At the same time, all Charley could think of was if the chief of detectives was this up on everything, he might also very well be up on her connection to the deceased police officer. Unlike the Cavanaughs, who seemed to be in every department, neither she nor Matt talked about their relationship and they did have different surnames, so the connection wasn't immediately made. But someone as sharp as the chief of Ds could have unearthed that sort of information with very little effort.

Charley felt herself fidgeting inside, waiting for a shoe to drop—or an ax to fall.

"Does this have anything to do with Jacobs?" Brian prodded when neither person in his office said anything further.

Even as he asked, he glanced at his watch again. He had a budget meeting to get to—it was the least favorite part about this job of his. He had a battle ahead of him, not one he relished.

"In a manner of speaking," Declan responded. "I'm short one partner—" He could see he was saying nothing that the chief didn't already know. Still, the request had to be formally made to someone in authority. "—and Detective Randolph volunteered to help with the investigation. Ordinarily," he quickly explained, "we'd put this to the lieutenant but inasmuch as he's not here and might not be tomorrow, I thought we should ask someone with the authority to grant permission—or veto it," Declan added after a beat, feeling that he should in all fairness.

Brian turned to look at the young woman in his office, his expression thoughtful as he studied her. "Why do you want to work this case?" he asked her quietly.

Her gut told her that the man could see through lies. Charley realized that she was about to verbally walk a tightrope. She did it very carefully.

"I was the first one on the scene," she told him,

"I found the victim's body and I thought—well, that I might be useful in the long run, being able to tie in what I saw to perhaps trap the killer."

Brian appeared interested in her reasoning. "You have total recall?" he asked.

She was pretty good about remembering details, but she wasn't perfect, which was what she thought he was asking about. "Total enough," she replied.

Brian laughed, clearly tickled by her response. "Honest," he pronounced. "Good. All right, since you're shorthanded and for once, the narcotics division seems to be fairly caught up, Detective Randolph is free to work the case with you." And then the smile faded from his lips as he leveled his gaze at his nephew and Declan's new, temporary partner. "I want whoever's responsible caught and faster than our usual time. No one kills one of our own and gets away with it."

"Understood, sir," Charley readily agreed. "We'll get whoever did this." She made the promise with zeal, not just to the chief of detectives, but to her brother, as well.

"And now," Brian informed them, rising from his chair, "if there's nothing else, I'm afraid I have to cut this short."

"No, nothing else, sir," Declan told his uncle, already backing out of the room.

"Thank you, sir," Charley felt compelled to say before she followed Declan out.

Brian looked after them for a moment. He knew he was bending the rules, but he kept that to himself. Because he knew how he would have felt in Randolph's place. Rules were there for a reason— but blood had a way of winning out and nobody knew that better than a Cavanaugh.

"I had no idea that he was such a nice man," Charley commented as they got into the elevator at the end of the hall.

Declan pressed the button for the ground floor. "Yeah, he's one of the few who remember what it was like, coming up through the ranks. A lot of other guys suddenly get amnesia when they get to the top, see it as an opportunity to lord it over the rank and file beneath them, but the chief of Ds is a real regular guy."

He wasn't aware that there was a touch of pride in his voice as he said what he did—but Charley was. She heard it loud and clear. She wondered if he cashed in on the connection every now and then. It would have placed a lot of people in his debt, she thought. He didn't strike her as the type to do that, but then she really didn't know him all that well. "Well, not *too* regular," she pointed out. "He is, after all, the man in charge."

And, as such, she'd noted, the man did have quite an aura, casting a shadow that was even larger than his tall stature would have ordinarily warranted.

Declan laughed under his breath. "He is that," he agreed.

Stopping short just after they left the building via the rear exit, he looked at his temporary partner as a thought hit him.

"Hey, you hungry?" he asked her, realizing that they had worked through lunch, a fact that his stomach was now rather impatiently reminding him of.

Charley shook her head. "Not really."

Seeing Matt like that, his life ebbed away before she had managed to find him and to possibly try to save him, had completely wiped out any trace of an appetite she might have had.

Most likely her appetite was wiped out for days to come, Charley judged. It was going to take a lot to erase that image from her mind.

Declan had never been one to quietly accept things he felt were wrong, even minor things. "You want to work with me, you've got to eat," he informed her simply, taking a serious tone. "I'm not going to have you suddenly keeling over on me because you're suffering from malnutrition."

She opened her mouth to protest, but didn't get the chance.

"We can get something to go, eat on the way," he suggested. "You won't even notice you're eating." He added, "I'm buying," thinking that might be the added incentive she needed.

Arguing with him wasn't going to get her anywhere, Charley decided. And besides, she got what she wanted—she was on the case, allowed to work it in the open rather than covertly. She didn't want to seem as if she was giving him a hard time over something that obviously seemed to matter to him.

"Okay," she relented.

"Great, what's your pleasure?" he asked as he began to walk toward his car again.

The wording threw her. If she didn't know any better, she would have said he was talking about… "What?" she said rather than wonder and come to the wrong conclusion.

"Food," he said pointedly. "What kind do you like? Chinese, Thai, Italian, Mexican…?" He let his voice trail off as he looked at her, waiting.

She wasn't hungry. She certainly wasn't going to be fussy. Charley shook her head. "Doesn't matter. Whatever you want is fine."

He had his doubts about that. In his experience, *everyone* had some sort of a preference when it came to food. But he wasn't going to attempt to coax it out of her. He had a feeling there would be bigger things to butt heads over before this case was solved.

He opened the door on the driver's side and got in, waiting for her to follow suit.

"Okay," he said, once she'd settled in, "I'll do the ordering."

Charley nodded, and then, sitting back, she asked, "Where are we going?"

Declan started up the car. "You mean what restaurant?"

"No, you said we'd get something to go, eat on the way," she reminded him. "On the way to what? What's our next stop?"

She really was eager to work this case, wasn't she? He supposed the chief of Ds encouragement to get the shooter responsible for Holt's murder sooner than later didn't exactly contribute to taking a laid-back approach to this investigation, either.

He took a sharp right at the end of the block. "I thought we'd canvas the area around Holt's house, talk to some of the people in the neighborhood. See if maybe anyone heard any loud voices, arguing or saw anything unusual around the time that Holt was murdered." According to his father's findings so far, the victim's liver temperature had placed the time of death somewhere late last night, not this morning as they had first thought.

Charley nodded numbly, wondering if she was ever going to get used to that, to knowing that her brother had been killed while she was most likely watching TV? To knowing that she wouldn't hear his voice anymore, wouldn't see that lopsided grin of his anymore.

Ever.

How was she going to be able to face each day,

to get *through* each day, knowing that she was all alone in the world now?

"Sounds good," she heard herself saying, only because she knew Declan was waiting for some sort of a response from her. And the longer she took to answer him, the greater the odds were of his noticing just how very upset she was.

"Okay," he said, nodding, "but first things first."

"First" turned out to be stopping by a Mexican restaurant that was barely more than a hole in the wall, a storefront establishment whose owner spent all his time cooking and preparing and none of his time involved in the upkeep of his property or worrying about its image. The man who went by one name—Ortega—relied strictly on word of mouth from his customers. And the word was *good*.

A deceptively sleepy-eyed old woman, who might have been either his mother or his grandmother, served as the cashier, seemingly coming alive the moment their take-out order was ready. She muttered a price to Declan which might or might not have been in English.

All Charley knew was that the woman's voice was so low, the words so garbled, she could have been speaking in any language. But Declan apparently understood her.

Either that or he knew the prices by heart and had the right amount to give her from the beginning.

As they left the tiny establishment, Declan handed

one of the two bags he'd been given to her. As she took it, Charley noticed that even the paper felt warm.

She couldn't place the aroma. "What is it?" she asked.

Declan got back into the car and began to drive. He spared Charley a glance. "Try it. You'll like it," he told her. He was being deliberately mysterious and he knew it.

Charley laughed shortly. "That argument didn't work for Tommy Mason in the tenth grade and it's not going to work now."

The sudden image of a teenaged Charley decking some overly hormonal suitor and standing over him, threatening to do more harm if he tried anything further, had him laughing.

"Tommy Mason, huh?" Declan asked when he finally stopped laughing. "So, did he turn out to be your first love?"

"I said the line didn't work for him," she said pointedly. Opening the bag, she looked inside. "You're not paying attention, Detective."

Declan pulled over into a large parking lot on the next block. The lot was buffered by a discount furniture store on one end and a chain pharmacy on the other.

When he turned off the engine, she looked at him with confusion. "Why are we stopping?"

"Because the first few bites require using both hands," he explained.

He took out something steaming and wrapped in wax paper. Whatever it was, it was beginning to smell pretty good, even to someone with no appetite. Seeing Declan taking a healthy-sized bite and neither tearing up nor having any sort of a coughing fit because the food was overly spicy, Charley decided to chance taking a bite out of her own portion.

Emulating Declan, she peeled back the wax paper, but rather than take a large bite, she took a small one.

The moment she did, she knew she'd made a mistake. Her eyes immediately began to tear up and her mouth felt as if she'd just bitten into a handful of red hot peppers on steroids.

Rather than diminish, the burning sensation seemed to increase by the second. She grabbed at one of the bottles of water Declan had bought when he'd purchased the two lunches. Popping the top, she consumed almost half the bottle in under thirty seconds.

Only then did the fire in her mouth *begin* to feel as if it was receding.

Sensing she'd just had a practical joke played on her, Charley glared at her new partner. "What *was* that?"

"Ortega's specialty," he told her.

"His specialty is setting people on fire from the

inside out?" she demanded, more than a little annoyed.

Charley liked always being in control. She didn't like losing her composure around people, even when it involved something so minor as being caught off guard by an overly spicy meal.

He laughed, really amused at her reaction. "You're exaggerating."

"No, I'm not even beginning to do it justice," she informed him. Rewrapping it, she deposited her so-called lunch back into the bag it had come from. "Seriously, how can you eat that?" she asked.

He found the meal a little spicy, but certainly nothing he couldn't handle. Declan shrugged in answer to her question. "A cast-iron stomach, I guess."

"More like an asbestos-lined mouth," she quipped with feeling. Her own mouth still felt as if it was smoldering. She drained the rest of her water, still feeling the effects of the one bite she'd taken.

Had they not been partnered, he would have told her that she was free to try it out and see for herself whether or not his mouth was lined with asbestos—because she most certainly looked as if she could deliver the heat.

But they *were* partnered, which meant that he had to behave himself and not let his mind wander in directions it ordinarily felt very comfortable wandering in. However, because things were the way they were, he had to refrain from "business as usual."

And, as a newly minted Cavanaugh, he felt he had things to prove, not the least of which was that he could conduct himself professionally no matter what sort of temptation he was confronted with or how close by it turned out to be.

In this particular case, he couldn't help thinking, temptation was sitting in the passenger seat right next to him.

Chapter 6

Everyone they found to question in Matthew Holt's immediate neighborhood was willing to talk. However, no one said anything that was even remotely useful—because no one had seen or heard anything out of the ordinary that day or the day before.

The woman who lived across the street from Matt, Kay Bishop, had noticed an unfamiliar car parked a few houses down the block, but her description was decidedly vague and she had seen no reason at the time to write down the license plate number.

"It's a good neighborhood," she'd immediately said in her own defense after telling Declan that she hadn't taken note of the license plate. "Nothing ever happens here, or at least, it hadn't," she amended, stealing a covert glance to Holt's house. Yellow crime-scene tape draped across the front door forbidding entrance. It stood out like a sore thumb. "I mean, the house down the block used to belong to a couple who argued every weekend, but it's been quiet since they moved.

"And Matthew was a cop," she interjected in a voice that said it was taken for granted that police officers weren't supposed to get hurt, especially not in their own home. "We all felt safe because of that. Who was going to mess with a police officer?" she asked. "It's a terrible thing, terrible," Kay repeated, shaking her head. She ran her hands along her arms, as if fighting off a chill. "I don't think I'll ever really feel safe again."

Charley did her best to appear sympathetic, but she was wrestling with her own problems in dealing with Matt's death. She had little left over to spare for a stranger.

"What it does," Declan told the woman, "is make you very aware that you shouldn't take anything for granted and that you should live life to the fullest every day. It also should make you realize that things that you mean to do or say shouldn't be put off to another day, because that 'other day' just might not come."

Mrs. Bishop seemed properly impressed and moved by what the detective had said to her.

She was still nodding her head, most likely mentally examining the meaning behind his words, as Charley and he finished with their questioning, walked away and headed back to Declan's car.

"That's pretty profound for you," Charley commented, looking at him over the hood of his vehicle.

Declan opened up the door on his side and grinned. "Impressed?"

"Almost," she allowed, getting into the sedan. "You've been reading Hallmark cards again?"

"That's cold, Charley." Adjusting his seat belt, he buckled up and closed the door. "You wound me to the quick."

She turned in the seat to look at him. Her seat belt clutched at her tightly, as if bracing for an accident. She found herself drawing short, shallow breaths.

"Do you and your wounded quick have any idea what to do next?" she asked, growing serious. "We've talked to everyone along the block as well as behind this block and come up empty."

His hands on the wheel, Declan hadn't started the car yet. Instead, his eyes swept along the length of the block they'd just covered. Nothing out of the ordinary came to mind. He hated when that happened, but no one appeared to be withholding information or lying. All too willing to talk, they were just not volunteering any sort of information that was in any way useful to their investigation.

There was only one course of action that came to mind at this point. "We go back and see if the autopsy yielded anything that might give us a little more insight into who killed Holt." He paused for a moment, studying her. "You don't have to come with me if you don't want to, you know."

She stared at him. That had certainly come out of left field. "Why wouldn't I want to?"

"Well, for one thing, autopsy isn't everyone's cup of tea," he told her. She had no idea what she was in for, did she? She struck him as someone who didn't have all that much use for caution, who went charging in just to bring the element of surprise to her opponent's doorstep.

Charley sniffed. "If I want tea, I'll get a tea bag."

She had all this bravado, but he still had a feeling there was this frightened little girl beneath all the gutsy rhetoric. Starting the car, he was back on the road again.

"You ever witnessed an autopsy?" he asked.

She couldn't lie, but she didn't want to say "no," either. So instead, she took the high road. "Always a first time," she replied, doing her best to sound philosophical.

Inside, she was trying very hard to harden herself, to brace herself for what was ahead. Seeing Matt the way she never had before.

It's just the shell, just the empty shell on the table. It's not Matt anymore. He's out, free. Matt's free now.

"Besides, the M.E. isn't going to be doing actual dissecting while we're there, right?" Charley did her best to make it sound like a rhetorical question, but beneath the blasé attitude, she was actually putting the question to him.

If she was asking, then he owed her the truth, Declan thought. "From what I gather, yeah, it's been known to happen."

His older brother had a great story about Bridget, one of his sisters, turning a strange shade of green the time she'd walked in on the medical examiner taking out a murder victim's liver. It was all she could do not to make a mad dash for the ladies' room when he started to weigh it.

"I could call ahead, make sure everything's back where it's supposed to be when we stop by the place," he offered.

She didn't want special treatment because he could use that as a reason why she couldn't come along, that she had to be treated with kid gloves. She was determined to pull her own weight.

"There's no reason to go out of your way," she told him.

He lost his patience. There was such a thing as putting up *too* brave a front. "Damn it, Charley, you said that Holt was a friend of yours. There's no need for you to see your friend in pieces if you don't have to. You don't have to act like some steadfast little tin soldier 24/7," he snapped.

It was an automatic defense mechanism. Charley lifted her chin. "Seems that you're the one who's losing it over the idea of walking in on an autopsy, not me," she told him.

"Fine, have it your way," he retorted, taking out his cell.

She realized he was still going to make the call regarding the condition of Holt's body, requesting it be intact when they arrived—and that she was being much too defensive, doing a complete one-eighty in order to make it seem as if she was unaffected by Matt's death and everything connected to it.

"You're still calling ahead?" she asked him quietly.

"Yeah," he barked. Then looked at her in surprise when she touched his arm as he was about to push a preset button.

"Thank you," she said in a voice that was hardly above a whisper.

He merely nodded, thinking it was probably safer that way. Charley was definitely not the easiest cipher to crack.

Sergeant Holt's autopsy had been completed by the time they arrived. Likewise, all the findings had been duly noted and recorded and were now waiting to be entered into a usable report.

"The lab results aren't in yet," medical examiner Dr. Donald Forest, a short, pudgy man, who seemed to be counting the days to his retirement, told them. "I can't tell you whether or not the officer was drugged yet, but I'm assuming so because there were no signs of a struggle evident."

For their benefit he reviewed his lack of findings. "No bruised knuckles, no skin beneath the nails. Death came from a single bullet, fired at close range. There was visible stippling around the wound so the gun was practically pressed up against his chest. And then there were the two staples in his chest," he barely mentioned, "but those were done postmortem."

The medical examiner wasn't telling them anything that she didn't already know. She'd taken in the single wound and had already decided that most likely, Matt hadn't been conscious when he was killed. He almost looked peaceful, not like someone fighting for his life.

"His blood alcohol level will probably come back rather high," she told Dr. Forest.

"He had a drinking problem?" the medical examiner asked, curious.

She had another way of wording it. "He had an ex-girlfriend problem which led to the alcohol problem. It wasn't something that was going on in his life for a long time," she told the older man. "He's not—wasn't—a diehard alcoholic," she said, correcting herself again. God, but it was going to be hard, thinking of Matt in the past tense.

The M.E. nodded as if he had expected the answer. "I didn't think so. His liver was in very good condition. Most likely in far better shape than mine is," he murmured.

"Text me the lab results as soon as you get them," Declan encouraged the medical examiner.

Forest gave him a rather withering, impatient look. "I don't text, Detective," he informed him. "I do, however, use the phone and I'll have someone here call you when I get the tests back."

Declan nodded. He couldn't ask for more than that. "Thanks."

A few more words were exchanged between them and then Declan took his leave, as did Charley.

Once they were back in the corridor, away from the drawers with their resident dead and breathing air that was relatively untainted with the smell of chemicals, he looked at the woman beside him. "You're not green," he marveled.

Charley wasn't going to point out the obvious, that there had been no disjointed body in view to cause her stomach to upheave. "Disappointed?"

"Just surprised," he corrected, then he shared a piece of his history with her. "I threw up the first time I came into Autopsy. Of course, the M.E. was right in the middle of performing one and he had a brain in his hand when he turned toward me. It was like a really gross scene out of *Frankenstein*. Not my all-time favorite movie," he confided.

"The original version isn't bad. It's melodramatic enough to be funny," she said matter-of-factly.

Her response surprised him. There was a lot about Charley Randolph that surprised him. "Old-movie buff?" he asked. He wouldn't have picked her to be one.

"Partially," she amended. She hadn't been, not really. It was Matt who used to get a kick out of the movies that were generally referred to as "classics." He would bring home a bunch of old movies that he found in the old video shop on Friday nights and they'd spend the weekend eating popcorn, watching old movies and taking them apart. And when it came to trivia about those old films, he beat her hands-down every time.

Charley could feel it again, could feel her throat threatening to close off, clogged with tears again. She did her best to shake off the sensation, occupying her mind with the details of the case and praying that they would, somehow, lead them to Matt's killer.

"What do you think the note meant?" she asked Declan abruptly.

Just at that moment, the elevator arrived. Declan waited for her to get in first, then followed on behind her. Reaching around her, he pressed for the floor they needed.

"What note?" he asked her.

She blew out an impatient breath. Was she paired with a detective who didn't pay attention? "The one that was stapled to his chest." It was hard for her even to mention that without wincing in empathy—even though she knew Matt hadn't been alive at that point and wouldn't have felt the sharp ends of the staples sinking into his flesh like tiny shark teeth. "Saying that this was just the beginning," she prompted further.

"Looks to me like we still have the same two choices—it's either a serial killer, boasting, which means we've got one hell of a bumpy road ahead—*or* the killer is trying to throw us off by making us believe Holt was just part of a larger whole." He regarded her for a moment. "You wouldn't know if Holt had been part of a task force, or was with a group of people who fancied themselves in charge or responsible?"

It sounded scattered and he knew it, but he was throwing everything he could come up with out there, trying to make something stick, something that could be vaguely connected to a motive.

But she shook her head.

"You don't know, or he wasn't?" he asked since what she meant wasn't clear to him.

"He wasn't—unless he was keeping it a secret from me," she said.

"Why would he do that?" he asked, sensing again that the relationship between Charley and the dead officer was a lot deeper than Charley was letting on.

They arrived at Declan's floor and got out.

"The only thing he belonged to was the police force," Charley said simply. "He wasn't a joiner."

There were joiners, and then there were *joiners*. "He didn't belong to any clubs, or organization, or church groups?"

"Nothing," she said in response to the first two things he'd mentioned, "and he wasn't a church-goer," she added, addressing the third item. "Said if he ever walked in on a service, the roof would undoubtedly collapse and he was actually doing a public service by keeping away."

Declan was about to ask her just how close she and the dead man had been because from where he was standing, it sounded as if they were *very* close. But upon reflection, all he would probably get out of asking her that would be a denial.

So he kept his peace for now, biding his time.

She had her own theory, such as it was. "Could be someone just hates cops in general and just happened to single Holt out, figuring he would make an easy start," she guessed, remembering the shattered glass on the floor. Had there been lipstick on the corner of the rim and she'd just missed it?

Was there something she was overlooking? Maybe, in an effort to forget about Melissa, he'd brought home a woman he'd picked up at a bar and she— Charley stopped abruptly. She was just grasping at straws now.

"In Holt's own home?" Declan asked her incredulously.

Charley shrugged, searching for a plausible explanation that didn't give her away at the same time. "He either knew his killer and let them in. Or…"

"Or…?" Declan prodded, ready for just about anything to come out of her mouth.

"Or the killer followed him home from a bar," she finally suggested.

Declan inclined his head, mulling over what she'd said. "It's possible."

Suddenly, the air was filled with the instrumental theme song of an action series from the late 1970s, early '80s. Declan's cell phone was ringing, trying to gain his attention—as if that theme song could be ignored.

"Catchy," Charley commented as the detective took his phone out.

He had a reason for programming what he had into his phone. "This way I know it's my phone that's ringing, not someone else's," he told her, taking his phone out.

Taking the opportunity to review a few things in her head, she gave Declan his space so he could

talk to whomever was on the other end of his phone.
Maybe even a girlfriend, calling to find out if she
could expect him over tonight.

Girlfriend.

What if Matt *had* come home with someone from
a bar? she wondered. If that was the case, would
it have been a stranger, or someone he knew? He
was—had been, she corrected herself, hating the
fact that she had to—a friendly enough person,
but sober, he kept most people at arm's length. He
wouldn't have invited anyone back to his house—
unless he was drunk and not thinking clearly.

Or maybe he didn't even know someone had followed him home and he had forgotten to lock the
front door?

She was accustomed to Matt being careful, but
alcohol changed people, made them careless, sloppy
and erased their memories or replaced them with
ones that had never happened.

The killer could have taken advantage of that.

But why Matt? Was it personal, or just a matter
of opportunity? Was Matt just a victim of being in
the wrong place at the wrong time?

Or...?

Damn it, all she had were questions with absolutely no idea how to get answers to any of them
right now.

You're going to have to help me out here, Matt.

Give me a clue, something to work with, she thought in frustration.

Out of the corner of her eye, she saw Declan returning his phone to his pocket as he turned around to face her. His expression was grim.

She braced herself. "What is it?"

"We just caught another one."

Chapter 7

"Another one," Charley repeated in an almost robotlike tone as comprehension of what the words meant eluded her—or maybe she just didn't want to let it in. "Another what?" she asked him.

"Body," Declan said. "We just caught another body."

There was only one reason they'd be given a second murder so quickly on top of the one they were investigating, and yet, it just didn't seem possible.

"And it's connected to Holt's murder?" she asked, a doubtful note entering her voice.

At this point, she was trying to figure out who could have hated her brother enough to kill him, and now, if what Declan was saying was true, it didn't have to involve anything personal.

Still, the idea that Matt's murder and the murder of this latest victim were somehow connected didn't seem quite right to her.

Declan nodded grimly. "The killer had the same M.O."

"You're kidding." The words escaped her lips quickly.

A half smile curved the corner of one side of Declan's mouth. Despite the gravity of the situation and everything they'd had to deal with today, there was something almost boyishly appealing about the way he looked. Charley was annoyed with herself for noticing. Matt was dead and she was noticing a boyish smile. What was the matter with her?

"Some people think I'm irreverent and don't take things seriously enough, but I never kid when it comes to murder," he told her.

Charley pressed her lips together as she nodded, trying to take it all in and having trouble absorbing the information at the same time. "By 'same M.O.' you mean there was a note stapled to this victim's chest, too?"

Declan drew in a long breath before answering her. "Yes, and he was killed with a close-range, single shot to the chest. But there's more."

"What kind of more?" Charley asked warily, trying to brace herself without knowing against what.

"The victim was another cop," he told her grimly.

"Oh, God." That was going to shake everyone in the police department, not to mention every relative of a law-enforcement agent, right down to their core. "So, you think that someone out there is deliberately targeting cops?"

Declan hated saying it, but there was no use in burying his head in the sand. It wasn't going to help catch the killer any faster, wasn't going to stop the killings, either. He'd make book on it. "Looks like that to me," he said.

Charley nodded her head grimly. "Then, barring a weird coincidence—" and she really didn't believe in those "—it looks like we've got a serial killer on our hands."

"That would be my call." Declan's statement was completely devoid of emotion.

"How can you be that calm?" she demanded. What was he made of, ice?

When he turned his eyes in her direction, Charley could almost feel his eyes boring right through her. "Who says I'm calm?"

Maybe there'd been a hint of something else in his voice as well, she reconsidered. Still. "You certainly *sound* calm."

"Because yelling and screaming isn't going to solve the case any faster or accomplish one damn thing. If it did, I'd be the first one screaming my head off."

Declan looked at her thoughtfully and she could see that he was weighing the pros and cons of an issue. Her instinct told her to leave it alone, that maybe it was better not to poke a beehive with a stick, but she had never been one to ignore what was right in front of her. Never been one to let sleeping dogs lie.

"What else is on your mind?" Charley asked, prodding him.

"What makes you think there's something else on my mind?" Declan asked her innocently. "For all you know, I could be reviewing baseball stats."

"Could be," she allowed as they rushed outside to his car, "but you're not. C'mon, out with it." Even as she coaxed, she braced herself, knowing that whatever was on Declan's mind, it probably had to do with her. Otherwise, he would have just said it straight out, wouldn't he?

Declan stopped before his car and looked at her for a long, thoughtful moment. "If you want to sit this out, you can."

She deliberately got into the car. He had to take her along, she wasn't about to be kicked to the curb now. "Sit what out? I wasn't aware that we were dancing."

"Sit out getting involved with whatever this is turning into. It's not just a simple murder anymore and I'm thinking that right about now, you probably feel you've bitten off more than you can chew."

Her eyes narrowed as she regarded him. "Well, if you had put any money on that supposition, you would have lost it. Don't worry about my chewing," she said, tossing his metaphor right back at him. "I can 'chew' just fine. And for the record," she continued, her smile vanishing, "just because I haven't worked a homicide—or homicides—before doesn't mean I can't. A decent detective is a decent detective, no matter what, and I don't have tunnel vision, I don't know how to do just one thing and nothing else." Finished, she asked, "Anything else?"

"Yeah," he replied, starting up the engine, "let's get going."

"You took the words right out of my mouth," she told him with a grim cheerfulness.

Victim number two turned out to be an eighteen-year veteran of the Aurora Police Department, a police officer just like her brother.

Officer Gerald Fitzpatrick enjoyed what he did and had no desire to take on the extra headaches that went along with becoming a detective. Being a patrolman suited him to a T. Of medium height and trim build, Fitzpatrick had been shot while still in uniform. He had put in extra hours in order to address a local elementary school assembly. Fitzpatrick had been one of the first to volunteer when the mayor had pushed for a program where police officers came to local schools and educated students of all ages about the dangers of drugs and alcohol.

Widowed and childless, Fitzpatrick had married again five years ago and was the father of a three-year-old son he doted on.

Because they were in charge of the investigation, it was up to either Charley or him to break the news to Officer Fitzpatrick's wife.

"You can sit this out if you want," Declan told her as they pulled up in front of the late officer's modest one-story house.

"Why do you keep trying to get rid of me?" Charley asked. He was probably trying to be protective, but she didn't want to be protected, she wanted to solve this damn case and hanging back on the sidelines wasn't going to do it. "I'm not *playing* at being a detective, Cavanaugh, I am one. That means taking on the bad as well as the good." If there was any good to be found in all this, she thought grimly. "Besides, you look as if you could use the moral support."

"I do?" Declan angled the rearview mirror down so that he could get a look at his face. "I don't see anything different," he said, straightening out the mirror again.

"It's more like your aura, not your face," she told him.

The laugh that rose to his lips was dry and it

didn't immediately call humor to mind. "I had no idea I had an aura."

"You do," she stated matter-of-factly, then added, "Everyone does," just in case Declan thought she was trying to do something inane, like flirt with him.

Aura, huh? Did that mean she was one of those "new age" types who was into herbal tea, and vibes and who knew what all else? He had no time for that kind of nonsense. "I'll take your word for it." He looked out to the door. Right now, whoever was behind that door was happy and he was about to say something that was going to change all that. It was a hell of a responsibility, being the one to ruin some-one's world, he couldn't help thinking. "Okay—" he opened his door "—let's get this over with."

But as he began to get out of the vehicle, Declan felt her hand on his arm, holding him back. When he looked at Charley in question, she said, "I can do this for you if you'd rather."

Why would she want to? "You have a desire to have someone remember that it was you who ru-ined the rest of her life?" he asked.

"You're not responsible for ruining her life," she argued. "You didn't kill her husband."

"But she'll remember that I'm the one who first told her about it." With that, Declan drew his arm away and got out.

Charley got out at the same time and quickly

matched his steps, accompanying him to the front of the house.

The moment she opened the door and saw the two detectives standing on her doorstep, their IDs opened and held out for her perusal, the smile vanished from her lips and Rita Fitzpatrick's face turned pale. Her dark eyes darted from one detective to the other and she asked in a hushed, frightened whisper, "Is it bad?"

There was no way to sugarcoat this. "I'm afraid so," Declan told her.

Charley caught hold of the woman as her knees buckled. Declan moved in quickly, taking the bulk of the woman's weight. The next moment, he'd swept her up into his arms. Charley pushed open the door so that he could carry the woman into her house.

He saw the sofa and made his way over to it.

"I'm all right," the woman sobbed weakly as Declan gently set her down. Conscious, she was obviously struggling to rally. "He's not coming home?" she asked pitifully.

"I'm afraid not," Declan told her. "He was shot leaving a middle school. He'd given a talk there earlier." The patrolmen who had been first on the scene had found nothing to help identify Fitzpatrick's killer. Neither had the one so-called witness who was still at the school, Donna Miller, a teacher who taught eighth-grade science whose husband was a cop. She was the one who had called the police, discovering the dead officer when she went to get her car.

A weak smile struggled to appear and then faded as the officer's widow nodded. "He liked working with kids, liked the idea of making a difference in their lives. He was the first one to sign up when the mayor came up with that program," she said proudly. "He always stayed until the last kid was gone, in case one of them wanted to ask a question and was too embarrassed to do it in front of the others."

That would explain why the school was empty when he was killed, Declan thought. "Sounds like a good man," he told the officer's widow. "I have to ask, Mrs. Fitzpatrick."

She looked up at him, confused.

"Did your husband have any enemies?" Declan watched her face as he waited for an answer.

"Enemies?" she repeated as if it was a foreign word she couldn't understand at first. "No. Everyone loved Gerry," she murmured, and then her face clouded over again as anxiety entered her eyes. "What am I going to tell our son? Michael's only three."

"You tell him that his dad was a very brave man who always made a difference in the lives of the people he came in contact with," Charley said softly.

Because those were the words that gave her comfort about losing Matt, if any actually could.

"Is there anyone we can call for you?" Declan asked the woman gently. "Mother? Father? Sibling? Maybe a friend?"

Numb, Rita nodded. "My sister," she said hoarsely. She began to recite her sister's phone number, then stopped midway, realizing she couldn't remember the order the numbers went in.

Declan was the very soul of patience, Charley noted with surprise. "Take your time," he told the woman. "It'll come back to you as long as you let yourself relax."

When the phone number did pop up, intact, in her head the next moment, Rita Fitzpatrick quickly recited it to him. Declan placed the call.

"How much practice have you had notifying next of kin that they'd lost a loved one?" Charley asked almost an hour later as they drove away from the small house encased in grief.

They had opted to remain with Rita and wait until her sister arrived to stay with her. The latter had been exceedingly grateful that they had been so kind to her younger sister.

"My more experienced ex-partner tended to inform the family. So, she was my first," Declan revealed.

"Your first," she repeated, surprised at the

amount of patience he had displayed. "Back in the academy I wouldn't have guessed that you had it in you."

"Had what in me?" he asked.

"Compassion. Empathy."

Back then, he seemed to be all about having fun. She'd thought that he would wind up washing out. He just didn't seem to be the dedicated type from what she could see.

Declan laughed softly to himself as he thought back to the way he'd been at the time. "Yeah, I guess I did stroll along the wild side a little too much back then. But that changed just before I graduated. When you lose someone, it changes you, gives you a different perspective on things," he told her.

He took the thoroughfare rather than use the freeway for the short distance they had to cover. He always preferred driving around the city, taking in the local streets to flying along on the freeway. For him it was rarely about the destination, it was always about the journey.

Declan was serious, she realized. Rather than verbally backing away, respecting his privacy, she had to ask, "Who did you lose?" She expected him to say something about a fiancée or a close friend. She hadn't expected to hear what Declan told her.

"You writing my biography, Randolph?" He slanted a quick glance at her before looking back on the road. "Because if you're not, then you re-

ally don't have any right to delve into the details
of my life."

"Sorry, didn't mean to intrude." She had that dig
coming, Charley thought. If the tables had been
turned, she wouldn't have liked having him pry
into her life.

"You're not sorry," he told her mildly. "But you
are asking a lot of questions and I still haven't gotten an answer to mine."

"What question?" she asked him point-blank.

"When we were at the academy, every guy had
the hots for you," he told her bluntly.

He saw a little pink creeping up her cheeks and
was utterly fascinated by that. He would have bet
money that women didn't blush anymore. Maybe
they didn't, but Charley did.

This one didn't operate under any standard rules,
he thought.

"But it was hands off because you were married.
I'm just wondering what happened to the person
the entire male section of the graduating class all
thought of as the luckiest guy on earth."

Charley began to laugh despite the kind of day
it had been. The laughter felt like a release. "Boy,
you still really know how to lay it on thick, don't
you?" she marveled.

His expression was the soul of innocence. "I'm
just remembering it the way it was, that's all," he
told Charley. "You made a lot of us lose our train of

thought whenever you walked by with those tempting, trim hips of yours." He rolled over the question he'd put to her and came up with his own answer. "I'm thinking you must have dumped him because no man in his right mind would have dumped you."

Charley inclined her head, deciding not to make a full confession of it all at once. Instead, she picked her words carefully.

"In a manner of speaking, yes, I did dump him. Because I didn't need him anymore." A suppressed smile flickered over the corners of her mouth.

"Wow, that's pretty cold," Declan assessed. Something didn't ring just right to him. What she was telling him didn't jibe with the woman he'd known back then. "You used him?"

She wasn't sure just how long she could keep up a straight face. "'He made a great shield."

He made a left turn at the intersection. "I'm thinking that he also had to be one thick-skinned guy."

Okay, she decided, enough was enough. It was time to come clean.

"Actually," she confessed with an amused smile, "he had no skin at all."

What was she saying? That she skinned him? That didn't make any sense.

"You're going to have to explain that to me," he told her flatly.

"He wasn't real," Charley told him. "I made him

up. If you remember, there were only a handful of women in that particular class and the guys were pretty persistent. I knew that if I didn't do something drastic pretty quick, I'd be swept up in the, let's say, 'extracurricular activities,' and studying would become secondary. So I invented Steven, bought a plain gold band at a pawn shop and became off-limits. It was as simple as that," she confessed.

"There were times when I did regret being married," she admitted, although she wasn't about to admit that *he* was the cause of the regrets she'd had, "but I graduated near the top of the class, so in the long run, it was worth it."

He was quiet for a long moment, digesting what he'd just been told. And then, still driving, he asked, "So you're not married."

"No," she replied.

Declan wanted to get this matter straight once and for all. "And you never were married, not even for a little while."

Charley shook her head. "Nope."

He nodded more to himself than to her. "Interesting to know," he murmured.

She had no idea what Declan meant by that, but she had a feeling she was going to find out.

And soon.

Chapter 8

"It's getting late," Declan told her out of the blue. He'd been silent in the car for several minutes now and she'd begun to wonder if he was annoyed with her for some reason. "Why don't I drop you off at the station so you can go home?"

She'd kept quiet because he looked as if he was working something out in his head. Apparently what he'd been working out was how to get rid of her for the remainder of the evening.

"And what will you be doing while I'm going home?" she asked.

His answer was honest. "I thought maybe I'd take a look at the crime scene. Patrol was the first on the scene and the CSI unit went over all of it while we went to talk to Fitzpatrick's widow, but I'm thinking we need to check it out for ourselves," he said, then quickly added, "Not that I think I'll see something that they missed, but you never know. Stranger things have happened."

She could see why he felt he needed to look the scene over for himself. What she couldn't understand was why he wanted to do it without her.

"And the reason I can't come along is—?" Charley asked, waiting.

"It's not that you *can't* come with me," he corrected her, "it's just that it's usually very hard to make out too many details in the dark. I want to look at it while it's still fresh and then come back tomorrow when it's light and things are easier to see."

The light changed too quickly and he found himself pushing down hard on the brakes in order to stop in time.

"But I feel kind of wired—" and the abrupt stop just now didn't exactly help negate that feeling, Declan thought "—and I might as well put that to some sort of use," he concluded, punctuating his statement with a shrug.

"Sounds like a plan to me," Charley responded. Nodding toward the open road before them, she made a suggestion. "Why don't you just drive to where the body was found."

There was no room for argument in Charley's

voice. She wasn't going to be able to sleep tonight anyway and it was too soon for the M.E. to release Matt's body so that she could begin making funeral arrangements. Going with Cavanaugh to the scene of the second murder seemed like a good way for her to keep busy rather than dwelling on her loss and what she could have done differently that might have prevented Matt's murder.

"You know, I don't recall you being this pushy at the academy," Declan commented as he changed direction. Making a ninety-degree turn, he headed toward where Fitzpatrick's body had been discovered in the schoolyard by a very traumatized eighth-grade teacher. According to what she told the first patrolman on the scene, she had opted to stay late to prepare the next day's lesson plan and on her way through the parking lot to her car, she'd all but tripped over the dead police officer.

Charley slanted a look at the lead detective. "Then I guess you weren't paying very close attention," she told him.

"Oh, I did," he assured her. "I did pay close attention." Closer than he'd felt he should have, since he, like everyone else, had thought she was married. But married or not, there had been a magnetism about her that reeled him in. He would have had to have been blind and deaf to miss it—and he was neither. He'd been aware of it even in the midst of his very active, very healthy social life.

There was something in Declan's tone that stirred her. Charley blocked it as best she could. She had something far more pressing to tend to than taking note of any sort of physical attraction between Declan and her. She had a promise to Matt to keep.

Still, Declan no-matter-what-his-last-name-was was one of those men who made it hard not to lose your train of thought once you were standing somewhere in his vicinity. She found that it took some effort to keep her thoughts focused on what she would have thought would have been the single most important thing in her life—avenging Matt and bringing his scumbag of a murderer to justice.

"Well, if you really *do* remember, then this shouldn't come as much of a surprise to you," she told him matter-of-factly.

Declan laughed shortly. "I guess maybe not." She marched to her own drummer, he thought. Hell, she marched to a whole other *band.*

But maybe that was where the attraction had come in.

That and a killer body.

And there was *definitely* attraction between them. He could all but *see* the electricity crackling between them, putting his body on notice that it was only a matter of time before something erupted between them. He was more than well aware of that.

Right now, it was like trying to ignore the elephant in the room, an elephant that was only going to grow bigger until he and Charley finally got together.

But not until this thing was solved and put to bed. And once they were no longer partners, then *they* could be put to bed as well.

The thought made him smile, if only for a second and inwardly.

There were candles and flowers and notes piled all around the area where the yellow crime-scene tape extended, forbidding entry. It obviously didn't deter the determined, Charley noted.

Declan seemed to read her mind. "I guess yellow tape doesn't mean what it used to to people these days," he observed as he slowly surveyed the entire area.

"People just want to pay their respects, let the victim's family know that Fitzpatrick was well thought of," Charley told him. This outpouring of affection would help the victim's wife—and eventually, his son—cope a little with the tremendous sense of loss which had yet to find the widow.

"Meanwhile," Declan complained, "the crime scene has been compromised."

Charley took a small, high-powered flashlight out of her pocket and squatted down for a closer look at the sections of concrete that were still peeking out from beneath the overflow of gifts. Squinting, she looked closer still. And then she shook her head.

"Can't compromise what never was," she told him.

He came over to join her, to attempt to see what she saw—or didn't see. "Meaning?"

She shone the intense beam on the ground, slowly sweeping the area on one side of the tape. "Meaning unless Fitzpatrick had no blood, this wasn't where he was killed. He was killed elsewhere and his body was dropped here." It was her best guess.

"Why?" was the first question that came to Declan's mind.

Charley lifted her shoulders in a helpless motion and then let them drop. "Maybe because this was the last place he made a public appearance. Maybe the killer was trying to say Fitzpatrick was a fake, only pretending to care about the kids he was lecturing to and he had to be exposed. I don't know," she admitted frankly, "but he wasn't killed here." She'd bet her pay on that. Rather than answer her, she saw Declan pull out his cell and quickly tap out a number on the keypad. "Who are you calling?" she asked him.

"Someone to verify your findings. If you're right, that would explain why no one heard a gunshot in the area," he said. And other than finding someone who might have seen Fitzpatrick's body being thrown out of the car, there was no reason to contemplate fanning out to question the people who lived on either side of the school.

The next second, hearing the other end being picked up, Declan turned away from the tenacious detective to talk to the person he'd called.

Meanwhile, Charley had taken several photos of the immediate area with her phone, preserving the evidence as she saw it and also to send on to the policeman's widow so the woman could see for herself how well regarded her husband had been in the community.

He was going to be missed. Mrs. Fitzpatrick needed to be told that, Charley thought.

Rising, she tucked her phone away again just as Declan ended his own call.

"You're right," he told her as he walked back to her. "This isn't the crime scene."

Well he'd certainly changed his mind fast, she marveled. "Who did you just call?" she asked.

"The head of the day crime-scene unit," he said casually.

She congratulated herself for not laughing out loud. "You mean your father."

"Yeah, that, too," he allowed. "Sounds more credible if I refer to him as the head of the crime-scene unit, instead of 'Dad,'" Declan explained with a good-natured laugh.

Charley smiled tolerantly, shaking her head. "You're too old to feel embarrassed about checking with your dad when it comes to evidence that he's processed. I mean, asking him is legitimate on your part. There are Cavanaughs throughout the whole department," she pointed out. "You can't walk without tripping over one or two of them. And from what I hear, it's not like you're still on training wheels and have to check with him before you do anything. You were just verifying information. Nothing wrong with that."

He watched her for a long moment, his eyes narrowing as they bored right into her. "You add 'shrink' to your résumé recently?"

Declan had managed to make a put-down sound almost like a compliment. So for now, she took no offense. She just filed it away for future reference.

"I'm more like a student of the human condition," Charley said, making a point of ignoring the sarcasm in his voice. It really was getting rather late now. "Okay, we've seen, we've verified, maybe it is time to call it a night and go home. I'll take that ride back to the parking lot now, thank you."

He'd offended her, he realized, taking note of her distant tone. He hadn't meant to, but he didn't like being examined under a microscope as if he was some large, single-celled plaything.

They were both tired and it had been one hell of a long day. Two cops had been killed today—and there might be more victims soon. It was way past time to clock out, Declan thought.

"You got it," he told her.

* * *

Charley didn't go straight home the way she'd indicated. Instead, once off the rear lot, she took a detour and drove one last time to Matt's house. Because of the hour, most of the lights in the surrounding houses buffering Matt's were off.

But she didn't have another round of questioning in mind, or even a quick reconnoitering of the area again. What she had seen at Fitzpatrick's mistakenly labeled scene of the crime had gotten her thinking and she wanted to see something for herself.

She wondered if she was going to be the only one who placed one of those candles within a glass container on Matt's front lawn. To that end, she'd stopped to buy one at a local supermarket.

The store, part of a countrywide chain, sold everything, including foodstuffs, cosmetics, toys and various other miscellaneous items. In the center of the aisle that dealt with things that defied labeling were items with religious connotations—like candles to be lit for the dead.

She bought one as well as matches and brought it over to Matt's house.

As she turned down his block, lights coming from an unusually low angle caught her attention. Driving closer, she saw not just one or two candles lit but more than a couple of dozen. Mixed in between the candles were cards, letters—some neatly written, most sporting almost illegible scrawl—all conveying sorrow and regret at his death. And love. Love tucked in amid teddy bears with drooping ears and black round eyes that stared back at the person looking at them. But in a good way, stirring up memories of childhood and a more innocent time.

Getting out of her car, Charley took her candle with her, lit it and then stooped down to find a proper place for it. She placed it near the center.

"You made a difference, Matt," she said in a low voice, tears suddenly forming in her eyes. This time, she didn't bother trying to wipe them away or keep them from flowing. The tears weren't hers to wipe away. They belonged to Matt. "And people are going to miss you, really miss you. And I'm going to miss you most of all," she whispered, her heart aching.

Unable to talk anymore, her throat feeling as if it was closing up, Charley lapsed into silence. She stood there for a few minutes, the lights from the candles gathered before the makeshift shrine to her brother bathing her skin.

"You made a difference," she repeated when she could, feeling very proud of him.

And wishing with all her heart that he was here.

Taking a deep breath, Charley turned away and walked back to her car, her heart warmed by what she'd seen even as it continued to ache.

* * *

Andrew Cavanaugh pushed himself away from the all-in-one computer in his office. When he had been the chief of police, before he'd retired early to raise his five children and search for his missing wife, computers were just coming into their own as a speedy way to get reports out. They even facilitated tracking fugitives—as long as nothing of a complex nature was involved. The information didn't link up to databases from other states. There were a great many gaps that needed bridging.

In less than ten years, it appeared as if the computer—and especially its research component, the internet—had grown exponentially until it seemed as if it was invading every aspect of absolutely everything. And while it made law enforcement's job easier on the one hand, on the other, it created a lot of the problems that law enforcement was challenged to work with and try to eliminate.

But tonight he had managed to do what he had been trying to do ever since his father, Shamus, had come to him with a problem wrapped in a request. Shamus wanted to find his long-lost younger brother, the child his father had taken off with to parts unknown right after his parents had divorced.

If this was right, Andrew thought, looking at the list of names his discovery had helped him compile, his father's young sibling, Murdoch, had given birth to a very active branch of the family.

There really *were* enough Cavanaughs to populate a small town, he mused. Maybe even a large one. Not only that, but the whole bunch of them had been practically under his nose the whole time, working at, of all things, a police force located only one city removed from Aurora.

Grinning to himself, he picked up the phone and called his father.

The phone, a landline, was picked up on the other end just before the fourth ring.

"You know what time it is?" a less-than-cheerful voice on the other end of the line demanded.

"Yes, as a matter of fact, I do. As I recall it, you taught me how to tell time when I was about three," Andrew answered.

The man on the other end snorted, clearly disgruntled. "Didn't I teach you better than to make crank calls in the middle of the night?" Shamus asked, sounding definitely cranky.

"Ten o'clock is hardly the middle of the night, Dad," Andrew pointed out.

"Depends on who you are and how long you've been up," Shamus countered.

"You want me to call back tomorrow?" Andrew offered, adding, "Maybe when you're more human and a lot more receptive?"

But Shamus surprised him by not letting him hang up so quickly. "You might as well tell me what's got you so excited you can't see straight. Seeing as how you got me up and all."

Andrew could almost see his father dragging his hand through his shaggy white mane, leaving it going every which way, like a man who had battled the wind and lost.

"What's so all-fired important that it couldn't wait until morning?" Shamus asked.

"You remember you asked me to look into seeing if I could track down your younger brother for you?"

"Murdoch," Shamus supplied the name, but kept a tight rein on his emotions, afraid of getting his hopes up and getting too caught up in what was going on this evening.

"That's the one," Andrew acknowledged.

"Hell yes, I remember. I'm not senile, boy. I remember. What about it?" he asked.

Andrew felt justifiably proud of himself. It meant, among other things, that he had a career back if he wanted it. He was still a pretty decent detective. "Well, I did it."

"You did what?" Shamus asked, confused. "Tried to track him down?"

"No, I *tracked* him down," Andrew corrected. When there was no reaction, he worded his accomplishment a different way. "I found him, Dad. Or at least I found his family," he amended, knowing that this was a bittersweet call with bad news laced through the good, because while he had managed to locate his uncle Murdoch's last known place of residence, that place turned out to be a cemetery. "Dad? You there?"

"Where else would I be?" the hoarse voice asked. "He's dead, isn't he? Murdoch's dead." The last part wasn't a question but rather a statement of fact Shamus knew he was going to have to accept.

"I'm afraid so," Andrew told him, but he quickly followed up with the good news. "But his family isn't. Seems that Uncle Murdoch was a very prolific man."

"What's that supposed to mean?" Shamus challenged, finding himself protective of the brother he hadn't seen in close to seventy years.

"It means that your list of Christmas gifts to your nieces and nephews has just tripled from what I can see."

Shamus's impatience came bursting through the line. "What the hell are you talking about, boy?"

"Uncle Murdoch had four kids—two sons, two daughters—who had a bunch of kids of their own. It's like a dynasty, Dad. You've got a whole lot of new people to meet."

"I've gotta see this for myself, boy," Shamus said. Andrew could hear the mounting excitement in his father's voice. "Hang on, I'll be right over."

And then the line went dead, just like that. It was his father's usual way of dealing with a telephone conversation. When he'd had enough or was finished, he just hung up.

Andrew smiled to himself. It looked like all of a sudden, ten o'clock wasn't the middle of the night anymore.

Chapter 9

The persistent buzzing noise finally penetrated the layers of disorientation that had wrapped themselves around her head. The low buzzing sound, coming from her back pocket, went off three times, then stopped only to begin again.

Her ears heard the pulsing noise, but it wasn't until her brain absorbed it that she realized someone was calling her cell phone.

Forcing open her eyelids—each of which felt as if it had been glued into place and weighed twenty pounds—Charley took in her surroundings.

She wasn't in her bedroom.

Slowly it came back to her. Because of all that

had happened today, she hadn't been able to fall sleep. But she was a stickler about avoiding any sleep aids to help usher her into a more relaxed state. So rather than pop some over-the-counter medication into her mouth, she had heated up a can of soup in the microwave and sacked out on the sofa, watching reruns of a popular procedural program.

Charley knew most of the episodes well enough to recite large portions of the dialogue verbatim, but there was something comforting about that, like visiting an old friend who could be counted on to come through each and every time they were needed.

Somewhere around 1:00 a.m. she'd fallen asleep.

When she opened her eyes again, there was a bright and all-too-chipper-looking news anchor on her TV making inane small talk with the traffic commentator about a possible trip to Las Vegas next weekend.

Unable to withstand such an onslaught of pure syrup so early in her morning, Charley felt around for the remote control. When she couldn't locate it, she stumbled off the couch and turned the set off manually.

On her way from the couch to the forty-inch set her cell phone began its buzzing routine for the umpteenth time. With a sigh, she fished it out of her pocket just as it began its third vibration.

"Hello?" she breathed, her voice sounding lower

and coated with the remnants of sleep first thing in the morning.

"Charley?" the male voice asked uncertainly on the other end.

"Yeah." The anchor and the commentator disappeared midword as she jabbed the power button on the side of the set. There was a brief sigh of relief as she dragged her hand through her hair, trying to pull herself and the immediate world around her together.

"Finally. One more go-round and I was going to have you reported as missing."

It was Declan.

Her new partner.

Temporarily.

It was coming back to her in snatches. Charley tried to focus on the watch on her wrist but her eyes hadn't fully woken up yet. Because of the program she'd just turned off, she assumed it wasn't seven o'clock yet. The brigade of frothy, so-called informative morning "news" programs hadn't begun yet.

"Just how heavy a sleeper are you?" Declan asked.

"Cut me some slack, Cavanaugh," she complained. "I didn't fall asleep until after one. What's so important that you felt you had to get in touch with me at the crack of dawn?" Charley managed to stifle a yawn at the last minute.

He didn't answer her question, but he did correct her. "Dawn cracked a while ago."

"Sorry I missed it," she murmured. Barefoot, Charley began to head over to the kitchen when she heard the doorbell ring. According to her reflection in the mirror, she was frowning.

Now what?

"Hold on a minute," she told Declan, banking down a wave of impatience. "There's someone at the door."

"Yeah, I know," he said. "It's me."

The last two words were said to her face as she pulled open the front door.

"Don't you even ask who it is?" Declan asked, his tone accusatory.

Blocking his way into her house, Charley turned her face up to his and asked brightly, "Who is it?"

"Very funny." Circumventing her, Declan made his way into the living room. Once in, he turned around and gave her appearance a once-over. Her clothes looked familiar. "Isn't that what you were wearing yesterday?"

"Is that why you came over?" What *was* he doing here, anyway? She didn't remember asking him to pick her up in the morning. "To critique my clothes?"

"I wanted to make sure we were color coordinated," he cracked, gesturing at her clothes. The humor faded as he firmly told her the reason for his appearance on her doorstep. "And to tell you that there's been another murder."

Any residual sleep completely evaporated the moment she heard the last sentence.

Holding her breath, she asked in a low voice, "Another patrolman?"

He shook his head. "The killer just broadened his base. This one just made detective."

Maybe the killer hadn't broadened his base so much as he'd been uninformed. "How long ago did this latest victim make detective?"

Declan thought for a minute. "I think his C.O. said it just happened a month ago." He didn't see why that was important—which wasn't to say that it wasn't, he realized. "Why?"

But she was clearly in her own world, weighing things, juggling timelines. "A month ago," she repeated. And then her eyes darted up to connect with Declan's. "The shooter might not have known about the promotion."

He was willing to concede that part of it. But where was she going with this? "So, what are you saying, exactly?"

She picked out what was probably the best theory, though far from the only one. "That maybe our shooter is a cop wannabe who washed out for one reason or another, or maybe flunked the interview, and he holds these policemen responsible for being turned away for some reason. If he wanted to join badly enough, in his mind he's blaming these men for destroying his dream and now he's getting his revenge."

"In other words, he's a nut-job," Declan summed up.

"I think we've already established that part of it," she said.

"We need to see if these men are connected in any way, then." He mapped out their next course of action. And then he smiled his approval. She was turning out to be pretty good at this. "Not bad, Charley, not bad at all."

"Gee, thanks, coach," she responded, deliberately pasting on a wide grin.

Okay, maybe he'd sounded a little patronizing, Declan realized, but he hadn't meant anything by it. He was going to say as much, then decided that it was better to drop the subject. There was no telling where that could lead and right now, her feelings and his inability to communicate correctly weren't what was important. They needed to catch this killer.

He scrutinized Charley for a long moment, assessing her condition. She still looked about half-asleep. He needed her fully awake.

His first inclination when he'd heard about the third murder was just to take off and investigate it on his own, but he didn't want her to think he was shutting her out. When he couldn't get her on the phone, he came in person to see what was going on.

Now that he was here, he wasn't leaving without her.

"How long is it going to take for you to get ready?" he asked. Before she could answer, he had another question for her. "You think you could make it fast?"

Charley banked down the urge to give him a flippant answer. After all, the man *had* stopped by for her rather than handling the investigation alone so she supposed she owed him for that.

"What's your definition of *fast?*" she asked.

For some reason, the word *fast* produced an image of the two of them, their bodies entwined. It flashed through his head, coming like a bolt out of nowhere. His subconscious working overtime, he supposed.

"We'll talk about that sometime," he told her with a grin.

It was a remark she felt was best left untouched. Turning on her heel, she mumbled something about being right down, and then she hurried away up the stairs.

Charley showered and got dressed in what amounted to record time, even for her—and she had never been one to dawdle. When she came downstairs less than fifteen minutes later, it was to the sound of the coffeemaker going through its paces.

The rich aroma found her first.

She stopped on the bottom step, taking a deep breath, relishing the scent.

"Are you making coffee?" she asked as she hurried into the kitchen.

She was still holding her shoes in her hand. It took Charley a minute to get those on and she didn't want to unnecessarily waste any time. What she did want was to sample the coffee in hopes that it tasted half as good as it smelled.

Declan turned from the coffeemaker and looked at her, clearly surprised that she was down here rather than still in her bathroom, getting ready.

"You're finished?" he marveled, even though he could see that she was.

"Yes, why?" Putting her shoes down on the floor, she stepped into them, then secured the straps. "You look surprised."

"I am," he freely admitted. He knew a lot of women and had had occasion to watch most of them get ready in the morning. To his recollection, not a one could even come close to matching Charley's time, much less beating it. "Most of the women I know take around forty-five minutes to get ready—except for my sisters, I guess."

All three were detectives on the force and he'd always thought of them as exceptionally quick. Not a one of them held a candle to Charley—not that he was going to mention anything of the kind to any of them. Women reacted unpredictably when they thought you were comparing them—even sisters, he'd discovered.

He was staring at her hair, Charley realized. Why? "What's the matter?" she asked, fingering the ends of her hair. "Did I leave some of the shampoo in?"

"No," he told her. "I'm just noticing that your hair's a little damp in places."

And that it curled appealing along her hairline and the nape of her neck, he added silently. The next second, he was upbraiding himself because that had absolutely nothing to do with finding their cop killer which was his single and *only* priority at the moment.

"Hair dryer's on its way out," she explained, dismissing the topic with a preoccupied shrug. "Why did you make me coffee?" Declan still hadn't answered that question.

"I thought it was the least I could do, seeing as how I woke you up."

Was that it, or was there more to it? *You're making too big a deal out of a cup of coffee, idiot,* she admonished herself.

Outwardly, she was fairly certain she looked casual about it as she shrugged. "You didn't have to. We could have stopped to get some on our way to the crime scene." She turned her attention to the only thing that was supposed to matter. "Are we sure it's the same guy?"

Declan was unshakable in this. "It's the same guy. Same M.O."

"He left a note?" If it was the same killer, he would have left a note.

When Declan nodded, she felt a slight chill descending over her heart. She hated this part of it even as she acknowledged that it might help in capturing the man sooner than later.

"What did the note say?"

He knew the short message by heart. "You guys can't catch a cold," he recited.

Charley laughed shortly. "Pretty cocky," she assessed.

Declan nodded. "That's my take on it."

"Well, that's good, isn't it?" she pressed, wanting to find out why Declan didn't seem happier about the turn of events than he was.

"And why do you think that's good?" he asked her, though he knew the answer. He just liked to listen to her.

"If he's cocky, that means he thinks he's better, smarter than the rest of us. Too much confidence never works out well for the perpetrator. It's just a matter of time before he does something stupid, makes a careless mistake and slips up. And when he does—we've got him," she said with relish as she anticipated putting an end to this monster's killing spree.

Declan handed her her prize. The steaming mug of coffee, topped off with a shot of creamer. "You think pretty well on your feet for someone who hasn't been up all that long."

She took the mug from him using both hands and drank almost half the contents in one long pull.

God, that felt good. She was almost human instead of a pile of free-floating electrons and neutrons, searching for a home, for somewhere to set up housekeeping.

"Maybe you inspire me," she said in response to the compliment he'd given her.

It was a playful, throwaway line uttered by a woman who was still a little sleepy to a man she'd known off and on—mostly off—for a number of years. There wasn't supposed to be anything about what she'd said that was the least bit intriguing or compelling or even have a ring of truth to it.

And yet, there was something, something he couldn't put his finger on, that seemed to have a life of its own and that life was operating independently of either one of them.

A life, he had a feeling, that was going to wind up making some sort of demands on both of them. Not now, not today or even tomorrow.

But sometime.

And soon.

He could feel it and from the way she was looking at him, he had a hunch that she could feel it, too.

"That's a really good cup of coffee," she said, nodding at the coffee she'd just finished, employing a second long pull. Setting the mug down on her coffee table, she said, "Okay, I'm ready."

He was still looking at her, as if her words weren't really reaching him. Or maybe he was getting some kind of hidden meaning from them that she wasn't trying to convey, she thought a bit uncomfortably. The last thing she wanted was for him to think she was sending out signals.

"Let's go," she urged.

Feeling a little foolish, Declan nodded and led the way out of her house.

She paused to lock the front door, then hurried to catch up. "Where did they find this victim?" she asked.

Again, as with the first patrolman and even the second, it was within the victim's comfort range. "In his car. He was sitting behind the steering wheel, probably getting ready to drive away," he told her. "The way I see it, the shooter approached him in such a way that the detective didn't feel threatened or that he was in any danger. Had to be someone he knew or who he didn't feel posed a threat."

"He got that wrong," she murmured under her breath.

"Nobody thought anything of his being there

until someone realized that the detective had been sitting in his car for a while without moving a muscle. That's when Sergeant O'Malley went to investigate."

"He was the first on the scene?" she asked.

"No, the first on the scene, the way I see it, was the killer, then O'Malley."

She nodded, doing her best to unravel this puzzle as she approached Declan's vehicle. "What do these three guys have in common?"

He answered the first thing that came to mind. "They're cops."

She inclined her head. They already knew that. She was after something more. "Besides the obvious."

He set his mouth grimly. "That's the jackpot question. We get the answer to that, we get our killer," he told her.

If only, she couldn't help thinking. "Maybe we should start going through the records, see who washed out of the academy or had their application turned down in, oh, say the last five years."

He had a more inclusive idea. "Maybe we should expand that, push it back to the last ten years. Fitzpatrick was an eighteen-year vet of the force," Declan reminded her.

"But Holt had only been on the actual police force for the last five," Charley pointed out. Whatever happened that started this killing spree rolling—if it did involve these three men—had to have happened at the lowest common number, not the highest.

"You sure about Holt?" Declan asked, trying to keep his facts straight. "I thought he'd been on the force longer."

"I'm sure," she answered with finality. "Holt did apply to the academy earlier, but then he had to withdraw his application to take care of—someone." She'd hesitated because she'd almost said that he withdrew to take care of her. She'd been involved in a motorcycle accident. Her car had just stopped on a street corner when a chopper had come out of nowhere and plowed into her. She wound up in the hospital for weeks. And Matt had been there for her whenever he wasn't working. Matt was the reason she'd pulled through.

There was a catch in her voice for just a split second that drew his attention. Again he thought that there was more to this than she was telling him. He could feel it in his gut.

"Who?" he asked.

Charley lifted her shoulders in a helpless shrug. "I don't know, someone who was important to him, though. He felt it wouldn't be fair of him to put conditions on his attending the academy, saying he needed to begin by asking for time off, so despite how much he wanted to be a cop, he put his application on hold. He was like that," she said. "Dedicated to whatever cause he was involved with at the time. He didn't believe in shortchanging anyone."

She sounded as if she knew the first victim a hell of a lot better than she was letting on, Declan observed. Had she and Holt been involved? Was that why she'd been so insistent about being part of the team that was doing the investigation? He knew she'd deny it if he asked, but he still had to know.

Declan decided that he was going to look into it the second he had more than half a second's time to devote to it.

"Okay, let's get going before we start falling behind. I want to catch this bastard before he kills someone else," he told her as he started up his car.

"No more than me," she said, buckling up, envisioning catching the killer in her own crosshairs.

Nothing would give her more pleasure.

Chapter 10

The street where Detective Barry Warren met his untimely end was roped off for one block in both directions. It wasn't a main thoroughfare, but still a well-traveled through street and as such, the road-block was a source of major inconvenience for those people who were on their way to work. The street led directly to the San Diego Freeway. Those who needed access had to go several blocks out of their way to make up for the road closure.

Several police officers were dispatched to redirect traffic while the CSI unit painstakingly documented the entire scene. The medical examiner's team arrived to render a preliminary judgment as to time of death while Declan and Charley provided two more sets of eyes to look over the crime scene.

"What do you think?" Declan asked her after they had been there for close to twenty minutes.

When they had arrived, the detective's body was still exactly where the killer had left it, sitting still on the driver's side of his vehicle. Only after the crime-scene investigators had taken their photographs and he and Charley had carefully looked the man over was Warren carefully extracted from his car.

Charley stood back while the M.E.'s assistant took the body away. "He knew his attacker," she theorized. "Or at least, he wasn't afraid of his attacker," she amended.

Declan looked at her. Those were his thoughts as well, but he wanted to know what brought her to that conclusion. "What makes you say that?"

"The window on the driver's side was rolled down. Whoever killed Detective Warren approached him while he was pulled over to the side of the road. The person indicated that they wanted to talk to him and Warren obliged by rolling down his window. The detective was shot at point-blank range and he didn't even see it coming at all. He wasn't on his guard, which means he either knew or trusted whoever it was who'd approached him."

Declan nodded. She'd summarized his feelings to a T.

"The killer had a hard time using his staple gun this time," Declan observed. "This isn't exactly the best angle to staple a note," he told her. "The other notes took two staples apiece. Look at the paper." He carefully held it up for perusal even though he was wearing gloves. "There are at least three other holes in it. The killer tried to staple this on him, but failed the first couple of times."

"Not very original, is it?" Charley commented. The words proclaimed, "You guys can't catch a cold."

"We're not dealing with Shakespeare," Declan agreed. "But to my knowledge, Shakespeare never killed anyone except on the page."

She looked at him in surprise. "You *know* Shakespeare?" He just didn't seem the type.

"Not personally," he quipped. "But I know *of* him. Why? Just how dumb do you think I am?" he asked, amused.

"Not 'dumb,'" she clarified. "Let's just say *ignorant* of the finer things in life."

He laughed shortly, shaking his head. "Let's just say we get back to the case," he suggested. "We can try canvassing the area."

"Because it's worked so well for us with the other victims," she said sarcastically, resigned to give it yet another try.

* * *

As before, their canvas turned up the same results as the past two attempts had: no one had seen
or heard anything out of the ordinary.

Again.

Two hours later, they knew no more than they
had when they'd gotten started. Declan sighed, exasperated. "I'm beginning to think our killer's a
ghost. Or one hell of a magician," he complained.

Charley had another take on the killer. "Or so
common and ordinary, nobody takes note of him."

Declan looked at his partner, intrigued. "What
do you mean?"

"People pass one another in a mall or a store
all the time without even being aware of them unless the other party looked or was doing something
out of the ordinary. Exceptionally good-looking or
very homely people get noticed. Average people
don't. These murders could have been committed
by someone you look right through, someone who
doesn't stand out or register—"

"Until it's too late," Declan concluded.

"Yeah," she said grimly. "For the most part, people aren't observant. That teacher who found our
second victim in the schoolyard didn't even notice
that there was no blood around his body and she
said that she was a cop's widow. You would have
thought that if anyone could be more observant, it'd
be someone who'd been married to a policeman."

Frustrated, Charley was dying to get back into the database she was working in. She had a feeling that the person they were looking for was there, right in plain sight. She just had a great many files to go through before she got to the one that hid their killer.

"If we're through here, let's get back to the office," she urged him. "I want to finish going through that list of wannabe washouts. I keep thinking we'll find our guy there—or at least I'm hoping we will," she admitted honestly.

Declan's cell phone rang at that moment, interrupting anything he might have said to her in response. Taking the phone out, he looked at the caller ID on the screen. "Looks like the chief of Ds has the same idea."

"What, going through the list of names?" she asked, not sure what Declan was referring to.

"No, getting us to come back into the station," he guessed, taking the call. "Yes, Chief?" he said brightly as he answered his call.

Curious, Charley waited for more, but her partner said nothing, only nodded his head a couple of times in response. "Yes, sir, we'll be right in."

"Anything?" she asked hopefully as he ended the call and tucked his phone away. Maybe while they were out sifting through clues, someone had come in and confessed, making their job infinitely easier—although somehow, she doubted it.

"Most likely," Declan replied. "But he said he'd tell us once we got back."

She didn't like not knowing things and there were already enough mysteries without having any more guessing games thrown at them.

"What do you think this is about?" she asked Declan.

"Well, it's not a surprise birthday party," he deadpanned, "'cause mine's in June and yours is—"

"Not now," she retorted. What was he doing, reading up on her? Or was this an attempt on his part to get her to blurt out her birthday?

"Nice dodge," he laughed, confirming that it was the latter. "Okay, let's get back and hope this guy has run out of bullets," he said, scanning the scene one last time.

The CSI unit was still there as were the medical examiner's team, but the latter was about to leave. Still, they represented two more potential victims on the move. "'Cause he sure as hell isn't running out of targets."

She knew what Declan was thinking. That any second, the shooter could open fire on them right here.

"He doesn't shoot into a crowd of cops," Charley pointed out.

"Yet," Declan felt bound to counter. "Who knows what this nutcase is capable of? He could change his M.O. whenever it suits him."

Declan was right, she thought. Not even two full days had passed and they already had three bodies. How many more were going to be racked up before they caught this killer? *If* they caught this killer.

When they walked into Brian Cavanaugh's office some thirty minutes later, it was evident that he was waiting for them.

Declan couldn't remember ever seeing the man look so grim.

Rising slightly in his seat in deference to Charley, Brian gestured for them to sit down. He did the same.

"I won't ask you how it's going because I know how it's going," he told them. "We've got too many bodies. One would have been too many," he couldn't help saying. The next moment, he was all business again. "I'm giving you a task force," he said. "No disrespect to either one of you, but you clearly need help."

"No disrespect taken," Declan assured him.

"We'll gladly accept all the help we can get," Charley said, backing up Declan's sentiments.

Brian nodded. He'd already gotten in contact with the detectives he felt would be most useful at the moment. He knew he was lucky because there were so many fine detectives to choose from, but many were on cases already. Still, finding good people to work this was far from difficult.

"Any new leads or suspects?" he asked.

"Only in a general sense," Declan told him. "We think it might be someone who applied to the academy but didn't get in for one reason or another."

Brian nodded. "In other words, he's looking for revenge."

"But it's also got to be someone who doesn't raise any flags," Charley put in. "He gets right up close before he shoots them. Once, he's lucky, twice, he's tricky."

"Three times it's a pattern," Brian said. "It has to be someone who looks nonthreatening," he agreed. And then he filled them in on the rest of his plan. "Everyone's on standby. Vacations are temporarily canceled, overtime is authorized. You're going to get three, maybe four more detectives to work this with you," he told Declan. "I want this over with. I want my people not to have to constantly be looking over their shoulders."

"Yes, sir." Declan took the words to be a mandate. Sensing the meeting was over, he rose to his feet. Charley followed suit. "I'll let you know the second something breaks," he promised the chief.

Brian smiled confidently. "I know you will."

When they got back to their floor, a bulletin board had been brought into the office. It had three photographs mounted at the top, equally spaced apart—for now.

Out of the corner of his eye, Declan saw Charley freeze before the board. Specifically, she was standing and looking up at the first photograph. Her unguarded expression was one of incredible sorrow.

Okay, this had gone on long enough. Declan wanted answers now.

The next moment, he saw three new faces. These had to be the detectives the chief had promised. That man worked fast, he thought, awed. As their presence registered, the men came over and introduced themselves.

"The chief of Ds thought you might like a little help with the grunt work," the oldest of the three said. "I'm Max Callaghan, that ugly dude is Mickey Sanchez and the tall guy behind him is Bobby Yu. We're here as long as you need us," Max told him.

Declan turned toward Charley. "Look, why don't you get these guys up to speed?" he requested. "Show them what you've been working on."

"Sure." She was more than willing to do that. Maybe between all of them, they could get through the files by the end of today. "While I'm doing that, what will you be doing?" she asked. Was it her imagination, or was he edging his way toward the door again?

"I've got something to take care of," he said. When he saw the frown that greeted his words, he told her, "Don't worry, I'm not leaving the building."

"Wasn't worried," she said, although she was a little. "Just curious."

He paused for a second, thinking that maybe he'd dumped a little too much on her all at once. "You can handle this, right?"

He felt something going inside of him beyond the customary physical reaction and longing. For a second, he allowed himself to examine the sensation and was rather stunned to realize that he was feeling not just the usual lustful reaction normal for a male when confronted by a beautiful woman, but also a sense protectiveness as well. In unguarded moments, he saw pain in her eyes. Not just the re-action that they felt as cops who viewed the less-than-sunny side of life. This was *personal* pain and he found himself wanting to make it better for her.

He was overdue for a vacation, he told himself. There was no other explanation for feeling this way—right?

It could have gone one of two ways. Charley knew she could have taken his concern as an insult to her abilities, or she could just take it as a display of sensitivity on his part.

For now, she decided to go with the latter. "I've been handling a lot more than you think," she an-swered, deliberately sounding mysterious.

That was just what he intended to find out about. He wanted to know more about her, know the se-crets she was keeping from him, because his gut was telling him that was what she was doing. Secrets that revolved around the first murder victim.

Nodding in response to her words, he hurried out of the office.

Rather than call down to the tech department, Declan thought a face-to-face request was best. With that in mind, he went down to the basement where both the crime lab and its offshoot, the much smaller computer lab, were located.

The door to the computer tech area was opened when he arrived, but he knocked on the doorjamb anyway before looking in.

Brenda Cavanaugh, the department's resident computer wizard as well as Dax's wife and the daughter-in-law of the chief of detectives, had her back to the door.

When he'd first glimpsed the woman at one of Andrew's get-togethers he'd thought she was a teenager. The slim blonde with the laughing blue eyes certainly didn't look like a woman who could make a computer sit up and beg as well as do tricks and roll over, he'd thought once he found out her name and put it together with the accolades he'd heard about the wizard in the department's tech lab.

She was busily working, her slender fingers all but invisible as they flew across the keyboard at speeds her husband said defied measurement.

"What can I do for you—Declan, isn't it?" she asked, never looking up from her work.

"They warned me you had eyes in the back of your head," he said with a laugh, coming forward. "But I didn't believe them. Maybe I should have."

Brenda was quick to squash the rumor in the making and fill him in. "No, just a good reflection coming off my monitor and an excellent memory for faces, which, given the ever-increasing size of our family, is an excellent asset to have.

"What can I do for you?" she asked, this time sparing him a glance. Her fingers never stopped moving.

On his way down, he'd worded this several different ways in his head. In the end, he decided that keeping it simple was best. "I need you to do a little digging into someone's background."

"In my spare time, right?" Brenda asked with a pleasant laugh.

"Actually," he told the vibrant blonde, "I'd like it as soon as possible."

"Is this part of the case you caught? The one with the shooter going after our own?" she asked. "News travels very fast here," she said before Declan could ask her how she knew. "And your dad's office is right next to this one," she said.

"In a manner of speaking," he said, answering her initial question about the query being part of the case.

"What's the person's name you're looking into?" she asked, pausing to pull over a pad so she could jot the name down.

"Charley—Charlotte Randolph," he amended, thinking her file most likely had her legal name on it.

Brenda stopped writing and turned from the computer to look at him. "Isn't she the one the chief authorized to work on this case with you?" she asked.

Already she knew more than he'd initially told her in his communications with her. "Yeah."

Brenda studied him for a moment. "And you can't just ask her?"

"Not if I want to hear the truth," he admitted. "I don't think she's ready to talk about it yet."

"Just what is it you want me to look for?" Brenda asked, watching him.

"I want to see if you can find anything about her connection to the first victim, Matthew Holt. When I casually asked if they'd ever dated, she countered with that old throwaway line about being just friends and wanting to keep it that way."

"But you don't believe her." It wasn't a question.

"No, I don't."

She resumed typing. "Why?" she asked.

"Let's just say it's a gut feeling. I figured if anyone could find out what I need to know quickly, you could."

"Okay, I'll get back to you," Brenda told him, turning back to her work. "And don't forget to take your shovel when you leave," she reminded him in typical-mother fashion.

"My shovel?" he repeated, thoroughly confused. He didn't have anything remotely resembling a shovel with him.

"Yeah. You did lay it on pretty thick just now," she pointed out.

"Didn't say anything that wasn't true," he told her as he left the lab. "And thanks a lot for looking into this for me."

Brenda's voice followed him out into the hall. "Don't thank me yet."

He knew she'd deliver. According to everyone, she was the best at this.

He didn't feel good about going behind Charley's back to get the information he wanted, but he needed to know if there was something she wasn't sharing with him about why she was so determined to work the case. Something that might ultimately interfere with solving the case.

Charley didn't strike him as someone who was motivated by ambition to make a name for herself in order to get ahead. There was something more at work here, something personal and he was already as in the dark about this case as he was willing to be. Any light he could find to shed on the different details, he was going to go all out and shed it.

* * *

When he came back into the office, he saw that Charley had appropriated desks for the three detectives that had been assigned to work with them. Not only that, but apparently she'd also gotten lunch to be delivered in his absence.

She looked up just as he walked in.

"You're back sooner than I thought," she told him. "I ordered lunch for you. As I remember, you liked Chinese food back at the academy."

"How would you know?" he asked, surprised. "You never went out with us anytime we were celebrating."

"You celebrated every Friday," she said with a laugh. "I turned up a couple of times. I just didn't call attention to myself."

That wouldn't have been possible, he thought. Her very presence called attention to itself. She'd had—and still had—a killer figure, a smile that lit up a room for a quarter of a mile and the bluest eyes he'd ever seen outside of an enhanced magazine cover.

He sat down at his desk. The aroma from the bag on his desk instantly reminded him that it had been hours since his stomach had had food drop by for a visit.

"Thanks." He began to open his bag. "How much do I owe you?"

"We'll settle up later," she promised. Her eyes were already glued to her monitor.

Chapter 11

Charley couldn't get away from the feeling that they were all sitting on a ticking time bomb, trying to find the killer of three policemen before he found another target.

For the past thirty-six-plus hours, she, Declan and the three detectives who had been assigned to the task force had been staring at five separate monitors, going through five years' worth of data. Data that concerned either any would-be police officer who had washed out of the academy for some reason, or any officers who had been terminated or forced to retire due to disabling injuries sustained on or off the job.

Given the length of time they'd been reviewing and the many different scenarios that the suspect might have been involved in, the amount of data they'd been faced with was almost overwhelming.

Shutting her eyes for a second, Charley rubbed the bridge of her nose. Aside from feeling as if she was going cross-eyed, she was holding one potential monster of a headache at bay. She didn't have time for a headache.

Mercifully, though she felt as if they were on borrowed time, waiting for the second shoe to drop, the killer hadn't claimed any new victims. Since the first three murders had been in rapid succession, Charley found herself entertaining the very thin hope that maybe the killing spree had ended as abruptly as it had started.

Glancing over toward Declan's desk, her eyes met his. "No news is good news, right?"

As if they were on an identical wavelength, Declan knew what she was referring to. He was also quick to point out the flaw in her theory. "Not necessarily. It just might mean that the body hasn't been found yet."

Charley sighed. "You are an optimistic son of a gun, aren't you?" she commented with a shake of her head. The fact that he might be right was something she didn't want to dwell on. "Is that why you keep watching the phone?" she asked him. "Because you're expecting a call saying there's been another murder?"

"I'm not watching the phone," Declan told her matter-of-factly.

Silently, he upbraided himself. He was going to have to be less obvious. Right now, he was letting his impatience get the better of him, waiting for Brenda to call him. From what he'd heard, the resident computer tech was usually extremely fast when it came to getting back to people.

Of course, it wasn't as if she had nothing else to do. When he'd gone to see her, the woman's desk had been swamped with requests and God only knew what all else. On top of that, she was doing him a favor, something that was off the books— which meant that the request he'd made could be easily bumped and sent to the back of the line as many times as was necessary until Brenda could find a few spare minutes to get to the information he wanted unhampered.

Charley shrugged in response to his protest. Maybe she was just punchy and it was her imagination. At any rate, the past thirty-six hours of hunting had turned up a few names that needed checking out.

"I've got a few likely candidates to talk to," she announced. Pushing her chair back, she rose to her feet. "I'm going to go check them out."

Declan was already rising, as well. "We'll go together," he told her.

Her eyes pinned him in place for a brief moment. "Is it that you're being protective, or you're afraid that I'm going to screw up?"

He grinned at her. "Which would insult you less?"

Okay, maybe he was just being helpful and she was being paranoid. "Let me think about it," she answered with a dry laugh.

The other three detectives had been busy compiling their own lists of possible suspects.

"Looks like we all get to hit the field at the same time," Bobby Yu said, shrugging into his jacket.

"Not all," Declan corrected. "You and Callaghan check out the people on your lists." He turned toward the third detective. "Sanchez, I want you to stay here just in case someone calls in with a tip."

With a shrug, Sanchez put his sports jacket back on the back of his chair. He didn't look overly happy about staying behind, but he had learned to roll with the punches no matter what direction they came from.

"Whatever you say, Cavanaugh."

Declan glanced in Charley's direction. "Maybe you should take notes," he suggested with a straight face.

"In your dreams," she teased.

Just as they were about to leave the office, the

phone rang. Sanchez picked up the receiver. After exchanging a couple of words with whomever was calling, the detective held up the receiver and called out to Declan, "Hey, Cavanaugh, it's for you."

The room became deadly quiet as Declan took possession of the phone. Within a couple of seconds, it became evident from his body language that the call was not about another body being found.

The call was the one he'd been waiting for. It was Brenda on the other end of the line.

"Sorry it took so long to get back to you," she apologized. "I had an emergency on my hands." Unable to go into details, she left it at that.

"That's okay," Declan said, brushing off her apology. He kept his voice low. "I figured that you were busy. Do you have anything?" he asked, aware that she could just be calling to say she was going to need more time.

"That thing you wanted me to check out for you?" Brenda began.

"Yeah?" Declan prodded.

"You were right," she said. "There is a connection."

He covertly slanted a glance toward Charley, making sure she wasn't looking his way. "I knew it."

"No, I don't think you did," he heard Brenda contradicting.

That made no sense to him. "What's that supposed to mean?"

"It means that Holt and your partner were brother and sister," Brenda told him.

"Explain," he requested, unable to put his question into more detail than that. Charley was looking at him curiously and he didn't want to alert her any further until he had all the information he wanted. When he did, he was going to choose the time to confront her with what he knew. He wanted this to be done on his terms, not hers.

"Same mother, different fathers," Brenda replied.

"Oh. That explains it."

"There's more," Brenda continued.

Something in the tech's voice told him the "more" was significant. "Go ahead."

"Seems their mother was pretty much a flake," Brenda said. "She took off when Charley was fifteen and Holt was eighteen. He was legally an adult, but she was underage. That meant she had to go into the system since there were no aunts or uncles or a grandparent to take her in.

"Holt stepped up and got himself declared her guardian to keep her out of the system. Then, when she turned eighteen, he got his letter of acceptance from the academy and was all set to go in. The night before that happened, his sister was in a car accident. The doctor told him that she was going to need a lot of care if she was ever going to walk again.

"He put his life on hold and dedicated himself to getting her back on her feet. She was his first priority and he worked with her around the clock, whenever he wasn't at any of the part-time jobs he took to pay her bills.

"Once she was back on her feet, he reapplied to the academy and got in. My guess is that she feels she owes everything to him. With him dead, she has no other family. Her mother never surfaced. I think there's a pretty good chance that she's dead."

Listening, Declan nodded to himself. That went a long way in explaining everything, he thought, slanting a look toward Charley. It also told him why she'd want her connection to Holt kept quiet. If her relationship with the dead officer came to light, she would be taken off the case since she was far too close.

He knew letting his superior—in this case the chief of Ds—know about this was the right thing to do, but he also knew how he'd feel if it was one of his brothers who'd been murdered. No authority, however loudly voiced, would have deterred him from carrying on with the investigation. At least this way, he could keep tabs on her.

Turning his back toward Charley, Declan lowered his voice as he made one last request of the chief of Ds daughter-in-law. "Brenda, can we keep this just between us?"

"Keep what just between us?" he heard Brenda ask brightly.

Declan laughed. For now, unless and until he decided to share this information with someone, the secret was safe. "Thanks."

"Any time you want me to forget something else, feel free to let me know," Brenda said just before she terminated the call.

"Another body?" Charley asked the second he hung up the phone. She held her breath as she waited for him to answer.

"No," he told her. "I was just following up another lead."

When he didn't say anything further, she heard herself prodding, "And?"

Declan shrugged dismissively. "It didn't go anywhere. But we are," he said, stepping up his pace as he headed toward the door.

Decidedly shorter than Declan, Charley had to practically skip in order to keep up. She did so without making any comment.

One by one, the list of likely candidates turned out to be less likely as Charley and Declan managed to track them down.

Of the five on the list, two had left the state soon after they failed to make the grade, choosing to make fresh starts elsewhere. A third, who had made the grade but then seemed to have trouble with authority and was let go, had moved on to a different career. He became a firefighter to satisfy his desire to live daily with a sense of danger, uncertainty and impending doom dogging his every move.

A fourth, Joel Henderson, had chosen a different career path altogether. When they interviewed him, Charley easily heard the bitterness in the man's voice. It seemed to be evident in every word and it immediately sent up red flags for her and, she saw to her satisfaction, for Declan, as well.

"So you hold a grudge against the department?" Declan asked conversationally.

"Wouldn't you if they made you feel as if you were a useless piece of garbage?" Henderson asked. The question all but throbbed with hostility.

"Not everyone is suited for that line of work," Charley pointed out as gently as possible, doing her best to bank down her own reaction to the man. She wanted to seem sympathetic to him in order to draw him out, and possibly trip him up.

Something about Henderson inspired its own hostile reaction from her. She glanced at Declan to see if he felt the same way, but his expression was completely unreadable.

Which, she supposed, made him better at this than she was. But she was working on it.

"Yeah, easy for you to say," Henderson groused. "You made it. Of course, you might meet with a bullet tomorrow," he mused, "so maybe I've got the better job after all." He laughed drily. "Nobody thinks about taking potshots at park maintenance workers."

Henderson had caught Declan's attention when the man had speculated about Charley meeting with a bullet. "Is that supposed to be a threat?" Declan demanded, his mild demeanor vanishing completely.

Henderson looked at him nervously, his belligerent attitude backing off. "No, dude, that's just an observation. Look, I've got to get back to work, so if there's nothing else, I'll be seeing you."

"Was that just a throwaway line or a promise?" Charley asked Declan after the park trash collector had put a little distance between them.

Declan's shoulders rose and fell in a vague shrug. "Your guess is as good as mine," he admitted, then asked her, "Do you like him for it?"

Charley thought about it for a minute. "He's an annoying jerk, but no, I can't see him having the guts to walk up and shoot someone point-blank— and I also don't see him as being the kind of person who inspires trust in others. Just the opposite, actually. He exudes hostility, if anything."

Declan knew that she was referring to the fact that Detective Warren had rolled down his window for the killer.

"Okay," he said gamely, returning to his car, "maybe we'll get lucky with candidate number five."

* * *

They didn't.

Candidate number five, a man named Joe Jordan, was no longer able to speak to anyone anymore because as the landlord who answered the man's door told them, Jordan was dead.

"Owed me two months' rent, too," he complained. "I was coming up to tell him that I was starting an eviction process if he didn't pay up. When he didn't answer the door, I let myself in. That's when I found him. On the floor, dead as a doornail."

Not exactly an original description, Charley thought. "How did he die?"

The superintendent frowned at the question. "Does it matter? He's dead."

"It matters," Declan told him, his tone deceptively easygoing.

It was apparent that the superintendent had been around long enough to know the difference between a show of indifference and the real thing. The detective, he knew, was not indifferent.

"Needle in his arm," he revealed. "Probably an accident." And then he went back to complaining. "Had enough money to throw it away on drugs, but not to pay me."

"I'm sure he felt bad about it when he died," Charley said, barely able to keep the sarcasm out of her voice. "When did he die?"

The rumpled man shrugged. "How should I

know? Two, three weeks ago, maybe. All I know is that I'm still trying to get that god-awful smell out of the apartment. Nobody's gonna want to rent it if it smells like someone died in it."

Charley couldn't find it in her heart to feel any sort of sympathy for the rumpled little man.

"Well, I guess that rules Jordan out as the killer," Declan said with a heartfelt sigh as they left the building and walked back to his vehicle.

"Back to the drawing board," Charley commented.

Declan could see she was more than a little annoyed and a whole lot frustrated.

In the interest of keeping him up-to-date, she told him, "I'm going to see if I can pull up the police report on Jordan. Maybe there's something there to help us—one way or another—although I doubt it."

"Maybe Callaghan and Yu got lucky," Declan suggested as he slid in behind the steering wheel. It took him a minute to wrestle with the seat belt that insisted on constantly twisting itself when it wasn't secured around his waist.

"Yeah, maybe," she echoed, but her tone of voice didn't indicate that she was harboring much hope in that direction.

She sounded beat, he thought. As were they all. "Look, why don't we knock it off for the day?" he suggested. "Grab some dinner somewhere and start fresh in the morning?"

Charley shook her head. She just wanted to keep going. She could catch a few winks, if necessary, right at her desk. "I want to see if I can find that autopsy report."

"Why?" he asked her. The car ahead of him was traveling well below the speed limit. He sped up to go around the rather noisy vintage Dart.

"Because I can't think of anything else to do right now, except go back to looking through the academy's washed-out candidates' files and HR's files of termination notices," she replied, a touch of frustration entering her voice.

"You're not going to solve the case tonight," he said.

She stared straight ahead at the dark road. "No, but maybe I can get one step closer to solving it." That was all she could logically hope for—one step at a time. "I just want to be able to get this guy before he gets anyone else."

"You're making it sound personal again," he said.

She saw no point in denying it. But she broadened the base. "Well, it is, isn't it? Personal to all of us? We're all cops, we could all be this nut-job's next target." She turned in her seat to look at him— or at least his profile. "Don't tell me you don't feel the same way. Everyone in your entire large family is a potential next target."

"Why are you shouting?" he asked her mildly.

"I'm not shouting," she denied, even though she knew she was. "I'm articulating loudly."

"You are doing that," Declan said, looking at her pointedly.

She could almost feel his eyes probing her, looking for something. "What?" she asked sharply.

It made her feel like squirming at the same time that she felt heat igniting within her, beginning in her chest and spreading out from there to all points beyond until she was almost fighting an urge to open a window and stand in front of a floor fan. What was going on with her? she silently demanded. Was she having some sort of a breakdown? Because, damn, she'd never felt quite this way before. This *had* to be the way Superman felt, exposed to kryptonite, she decided, searching for a glimmer of humor within the situation.

With effort, Charley continued blocking these thrusts and parries into her inner sanctum, but it was really getting harder and harder to do that, to remain strong and unaffected.

He debated saying something, but he wanted to be able to phrase it better than the words that were going through his head at the moment. So instead, taking a sharp right turn at the end of the block, he said, "We're going to dinner."

She glared at him. Did he think he could order her around like this? "What if I'm not hungry?"

Unfazed, he had an answer for that. "You can watch me eat."

"Yu or Callaghan might have found something," she said, which was a good argument for returning to the station first, not a fast-food place.

He took her protest in stride. "They have my number, they'll call. Anything else?"

Okay, they were clearly waltzing around something, but what? "Yeah, what's bothering you?"

Declan stopped at a red light, which gave him a chance to look at her for a long moment. Okay, maybe now *was* the time to ask.

Silence all but pulsed within the sedan before he asked, "Why didn't you tell me?"

Drop it, Charley. Don't ask, don't ask. This can't be good.

But she had always been like a junkyard dog with a bone and she *couldn't* just drop the matter. "Tell you what?"

"That Officer Matt Holt was your brother?"

Chapter 12

Charley considered playing dumb, but it was too late for that.

She also thought—fleetingly—of denying it, of saying she didn't know what Declan was talking about, that Matt wasn't her brother. But she just couldn't bring herself to deny Matt. To her way of thinking, Matt was the very reason why she was still here, why she was alive at all. He was also the reason why she had become a cop.

"How did you find out?" she asked Declan, her voice almost hollow sounding.

As hollow as she felt at times.

He brushed her question aside. They were partners and a partnership, however short, had to be built on trust or it just didn't work. "That doesn't matter. The point is I know and you didn't tell me."

Charley gauged her words carefully. She only had one shot at making him understand and she knew it. "If I had told you in the beginning that Matt was my brother, would you have even *considered* letting me work the case?"

He didn't hesitate. "No."

Her point was made. "Well, there you have your answer."

The look he gave her was flat and unreadable. Had she lost him? "And what makes you think that I'll let you work it now?"

Passion filled her as she pleaded her case. "Because you're a Cavanaugh. Because you know what family means. Because you can't sit there and tell me that if it was you in my place and some sick lowlife had killed your brother, shot him dead in his home, that you wouldn't do everything in your power to find the person who did it and that no rules, no person in charge could bar you from the investigation because *nothing* in the world was going to make you go home and sit on your hands, waiting for someone else to solve the crime." She was almost shouting when she finished.

He wondered if Charley was aware of how compelling she looked when emotion fueled every word she uttered. The word *magnificent* echoed in his head.

But when he spoke, he spoke quietly. "You sound very sure of yourself."

She didn't want him thinking she was conceited. That wasn't why she'd said what she had. "No, in the long run, I'm sure of you."

"If you were so sure of me, why didn't you tell me the truth when I asked how you knew Holt? Why the games?"

"Because, if at all possible, I wanted to give you plausible deniability, so if it came to light that he was my brother, no one could chew you out for letting me work the case. The fault would be mine alone."

Declan laughed shortly. "Got an answer for everything, don't you?"

"No," she told him quietly, "I still don't have an answer for who killed him and why—and I'm not going to stop until I find out."

Silence descended over the inside of the sedan, falling like an asbestos curtain for the second time tonight.

As each second ticked away, Charley felt edgier. Finally, she had to ask, had to know, "Are you going to tell the chief?"

Declan didn't answer right away. Blowing out a breath, he ran one hand along the back of his neck, as if that could somehow help knead out the kinks in his mind. The other hand remained on the steering wheel, guiding the vehicle to a favorite restaurant of his. He still intended to get something to eat, was still determined to have Charley eat something, as well.

"Hell of a spot," he admitted.

"That's why I didn't tell you anything," she said. "I didn't want you to have to wrestle with this. You need your mind free to concentrate on finding the killer."

He wasn't *that* gullible, Declan thought. "And you also didn't want me barring you from the investigation."

Charley inclined her head. "And I also didn't want you barring me from the investigation," she conceded. She looked around. The area they were driving through didn't seem familiar to her. "Aren't we going back to the office?" she asked.

"We're going to get dinner, remember?"

He was still willing to eat with her? Charley was surprised. She'd been positive that it would take Declan time to get over being duped. He was acting as if what she'd done was of no consequence to him. Was that possible? Could he be that thick skinned?

"I thought after I told you I was withholding information," she said, "you'd want to deposit me next to my car as soon as possible."

Granted, annoyance had flashed through his veins, but it came and went, especially when she pointed out how he would feel in her place. "Maybe you don't know me as well as you think you do," he countered.

Charley smiled, more than willing to agree—and to be grateful that she was wrong about him, that Declan wasn't just out for himself. The man could actually empathize with someone, something that she wouldn't have thought him capable of.

"You've come a long way since the academy," she acknowledged.

"How would you know about that?" he asked. "With your nose buried in a book, studying whenever you were actually around and not running home to that invisible husband of yours, you never really mingled with anyone, especially not me." And then he shook his head incredulously, laughing at himself. "I can't believe that I was actually taken in by your charade about being married."

They arrived at the restaurant. It was built out of large, rounded stones, and when Charley saw it, she thought it looked very much like the cottage where Snow White found the seven dwarfs. Easing the car into one of the parking spaces in front of the restaurant, Declan got out and waited for her to do the same.

"What would you have done if I'd tried to persuade you to hang around for a bit back then? If I'd tried to coax you into loosening up and having some fun?" he asked, curious and wondering if he'd allowed opportunities to slip through his fingers.

Was *that* why he found her so attractive? Because she was the one who got away and he hadn't even realized it back then?

She smiled at him, remembering a time or two when she had been sorely tempted to give up the charade and make herself available to him—but then, he'd always had some woman or other on his arm. Women seemed to flock to him and he certainly made no effort to hold them at bay. And she had never been one to settle for being part of a crowd.

"I would have told you that my husband was expecting me to be home when he got there and that I didn't want to mess up a good thing just to have one drink with you. But you didn't press," she reminded him.

It wouldn't have been just for one drink, Declan thought. It would have been for a memorable interlude. "I should have," he said, feeling a twinge of regret as he looked back at that period of time.

"No, you not pressing was one of the things I found appealing about you. You pursued me but didn't try to cross the line."

One of the things. She'd said "one of the things." Were there more? he wondered. Out loud he asked, "Others did?"

"A couple," she allowed.

The wide smile on Charley's lips told him there was more to the story than she was telling. "What happened to them?"

A fond note slipped into her voice as she referred to her brother and the close relationship they'd shared. "Matt taught me a few very good moves in self-defense. He wanted to make sure I could protect myself if the need ever came up."

As they walked into the restaurant, he could see her face better. She seemed very content with the story she was recalling. "And I take it that it did?"

"Just once," she admitted. "Ken McCarthy thought I'd change my mind if he dazzled me."

It took him a moment to recall the rookie she was talking about. McCarthy left the force after his first year, moving to Sacramento and joining the police department there. After that, he'd lost track of the other man, but it was no loss. There was something a little off-putting about the guy.

"And did he?" Declan asked. "Dazzle you?" he supplied in case she didn't understand what he was asking.

"He most certainly did not," she replied as they approached the hostess's desk.

After Declan held up two fingers, the hostess picked up two menus, flashed a smile at them and told them to follow her. She led them into the dining area and their table.

"Besides," Charley continued once she was

seated, "McCarthy was too in love with himself for there to be room for anyone else in his world."

Declan thought back for a moment. "You know, now that I think about it, McCarthy sported this peculiar limp for a while. He wouldn't talk about it when someone asked him what happened." He looked at her, amused. "You wouldn't have had anything to do with that, would you?"

Charley inclined her head evasively. "The man wouldn't take no for an answer," she said. "And I was fresh out of hand puppets."

Declan laughed heartily as he pictured the encounter. The man she was talking about was almost twice her size. "I would have paid to see that," he told her.

Still laughing, Declan picked up his menu and glanced over it. It hadn't changed since the last time he'd had occasion to stop by. Which meant he was getting the prime rib, as usual.

Closing the menu, he looked at her. "See anything you like?" he asked.

Charley raised her eyes to his. The question had caused a flurry of butterflies to take off in her stomach, completely surprising her. As did the spontaneous answer to his question that popped into her head.

Yes, you.

Charley told herself it was because she was just feeling vulnerable. Since she'd found Matt shot dead in his house, she'd been periodically ambushed by waves of loneliness that came out of nowhere and burst over her, making her lose her breath as well as her train of thought for a moment.

She was certain that the response had its origins in her wanting to feel less alone, to feel that she was part of someone's life. But getting tangled up with Declan Cavanaugh was *not* an answer to anything and it would create more problems than it solved.

This unbelievably painful, lost feeling would pass, she told herself. She just had to wait it out and stay strong.

Charley forced a bright smile to her lips. "What are you having?"

It took him a moment to replay her question before he could absorb it. The look in her eyes just then when she raised them to his had temporarily blotted out his ability to think.

He could have *sworn* he felt an electrical charge shooting between them and right through him.

He told himself it was his imagination, that he'd been pushing himself and getting very little sleep since he'd been put in charge.

He could tell himself all sorts of things from morning until night, but for the most part, he knew they would be lies. Because there was just something about this woman that fate and his uncle had coupled him with, something that went beyond a simple professional partnership. Something that was far more basic and far less structured than that.

The feeling was almost primal.

And he needed to keep it in check if he wanted to satisfactorily resolve this case and if he valued his career.

Charley leaned closer. He looked like he was a million miles away. Was he thinking about the case, or had something else lured his mind away?

"Declan?"

Her voice was like a magnet, drawing him back to the present.

"Sorry," he apologized, "got lost in thought there for a second." He recalled her question. "I'm having the prime rib." The second he said that, mentioning the prime rib with relish, he realized that among the things that he didn't know about the woman sitting opposite him were her food preferences. He'd just assumed she was like him. But a growing number of people weren't anymore. "You're not a vegan or a vegetarian, are you?" he asked cautiously.

His tone made her laugh. "God, no. I don't think I could make it through a week without some kind of meal involving meat every day."

"Okay, then, you'll really like the prime rib," he told her with enthusiasm, something he refrained from doing normally.

That was good enough for her. "Prime rib it is,"

Charley said, closing her menu just as the waitress returned with their beverages.

The young woman took their orders, promised to be back soon and then vanished.

Declan sat back in his seat, studying her for a moment before asking out of the blue, "Why'd you become a cop?"

As an afterthought, he picked up the wicker basket the waitress had left in her wake and offered it to Charley. There were rolls in the basket.

She took the smallest one and broke it open with her fingers. She took it plain. Declan, she noted, spread butter over his before taking a bite.

"Matt," she answered simply. "He became a cop, so I wanted to be one. He was always doing selfless things and I wanted nothing more than to be just like him," she confessed. "And to make him proud of me." A fond expression slipped over her face as bits and pieces of memories came tiptoeing back. "He used to tell me that I didn't have to do anything but be a good person and that was enough for him. All he wanted, he said, was for me to be happy."

"Sorry I never got to know him. He sounds like he was a great guy," Declan said.

"Oh, he was," she assured him. "He was."

And here they came again, marching out of nowhere, Charley thought. Tears. One minute she was talking to Declan, the next, she could feel tears gathering in her eyes, just like that.

Annoyed with herself, she mumbled an apology as she swiped at her eyes with the back of her hand. "Sorry. I'm not usually like this."

"Nothing to be sorry about," he told her gently. "Holt was your brother—and your only family— it's perfectly normal for you to feel the way you do. It'd be abnormal not to."

She looked up at him as he offered her a handkerchief. Charley wiped her eyes quickly, then handed it back to him. "Thank you," she murmured, embarrassed nonetheless.

Taking the handkerchief back, Declan tucked it into his pocket. "The M.E. is going to release your brother's body sometime in the next few days. If you need any help picking out a funeral parlor, making the arrangements, just say the word. I can help," he volunteered.

Then, in case she thought he was undermining her abilities, he told Charley, "Most people don't have a funeral parlor picked out unless they have a large family and have gone through this before. I just thought you might want a little help."

She hadn't thought of him as losing anyone. He was part of the Cavanaughs and as such, larger than life. People who were larger than life had no use for funeral parlors nor any working knowledge of one, either. They were invincible.

But obviously not, she thought. "Who did you lose?" she asked Declan.

"My mother," he replied quietly. "Chapel Hills Funeral Parlor is a pretty decent place to deal with—as well as reasonable."

That was what she needed. Reasonable. Charley nodded her thanks. "I'll keep that in mind," she told him and then went on to comment. "You know, you're a pretty decent person."

"And this surprises you why?" Declan asked, amused and curious at the same time.

"Well, to be honest, I got a completely different impression of you at the academy," she admitted. "Every time I saw you outside the classroom or the gun range, you always had a girl on your arm—a different girl."

"Just looking for the right one," he deadpanned innocently.

She laughed then and it felt good. "Thanks," she murmured when her laughter finally faded. "I needed that."

Declan smiled into her eyes. "Anytime, Charley. All you need to do is just say the word."

The waitress returned with their dinners. They waited until she was finished and had withdrawn before resuming their conversation.

They talked all the way through dinner, talked as if they had known each other well forever rather than just by sight or in passing the past few years. And the more they talked, the more drawn to him Charley felt, despite all the reasons she'd given herself not to be. She couldn't seem to convince herself otherwise.

Moreover, as they talked, Charley couldn't help but feel that Matt would have approved of this particular Cavanaugh with the wild, partially unfounded reputation. Because Declan was far more than just a really handsome man. He was a cop in every sense of the word. Bright, intuitive, dedicated and kind.

And she enjoyed his company.

A great deal.

And that, she knew in her heart, was dangerous.

Chapter 13

He drove Charley back to the police station parking lot to pick up her car. "Okay, now you can go home," Declan told her as he parked his car next to hers.

"Sure, in a little while," she said, getting out of his vehicle. "I just need to check something out first."

He was out of his car in a second, coming around to the passenger side. "It'll keep until morning," he insisted. There was no humor in his voice.

"But—"

Declan didn't let her frame her protest. There wasn't anything she could say that would get him to agree to letting her work even a few minutes longer. She was going to wear herself out.

"No 'buts,'" he warned sharply. "I want you home and in bed."

Declan wasn't prepared to have her laugh at the order. Just how exhausted was she? When he looked at her quizzically, Charley said, "Maybe not all that much has changed since your academy days."

Only then did he realize what he'd said and what those words must have sounded like to her.

As they sank in, Declan also realized that a side of him wouldn't have been all that averse to having exactly that happen: taking her to his bed.

Be that as it may, he needed to dig himself out of the hole he'd just created.

"As tempting as that might be," he told her, "I'm speaking as the primary on this case, not as someone who's attracted to you."

Her eyes widened. Was that another slip of the tongue? Or...?

"Are you?" she heard herself asking. At least, it sounded like her voice, although for the life of her, Charley couldn't have said where her question had come from.

The parking lot was deserted. The skeleton crew that was on duty had found parking in the front of the building. There was no one else in the immediate vicinity, no vehicles passing by. No one, he was acutely aware, to see them.

"No," Declan answered, threading his fingers through her hair just before he cupped the back of

Charley's head. The words slipped from his lips in a hushed breath before he lowered his mouth to hers and did what he realized he'd been wanting to do since the first time he laid eyes on her seven years ago.

He kissed her.

Everything that she had suppressed, all the emotions that had been stirred up the morning she'd found Matt and had remained with her, bottled up and repressed, burst forward now, surging through her veins and taking her entire being prisoner.

If asked, Charley wouldn't have even been able to describe what she was feeling, only that she *was* feeling. Knowing it was wrong, knowing this wasn't the time, the place nor the man she should be having these feelings for, she still couldn't make herself pull back, couldn't shut down because for one brief, shining moment, it was intoxicatingly wonderful to actually *feel* again.

What the hell was this?

The question telegraphed itself over and over again in his brain as Declan tried desperately to make sense of what he was experiencing. He was practically *born* enjoying women and had never, ever lacked for companionship. The exact opposite was true. There were times when he had to practically fight the more aggressive women off. He certainly wasn't a stranger to relationships of varying intensities.

But what he was feeling right now, what had suddenly risen up inside of him, was, for lack of a better way to describe it, *different*.

He felt like a man who suddenly found himself on a tightrope without knowing how he got there. He could see where he needed to be in order to be safe again, but the distance between there and here was definitely *not* insignificant.

He hadn't had so much as a glass of beer with dinner, yet his head was spinning. Survival instincts kicked in with a vengeance and had him pulling back—before he wasn't able to.

"Nope," he said in a voice that threatened to crack if it went above a whisper, "not attracted at all."

She had to take a breath before saying anything and then echoed his sentiment. "Me, neither."

Damn, what the hell had happened just now?

His knees felt weak, as if he'd made contact with a taser.

"Glad we got that out of the way," he told her, still carefully enunciating his words. His tongue felt thick and clumsy in his mouth, unequal to the challenge of managing long words. "Now get into your car and go home," he said. "That's an order."

"Sure. See you," she said. When he made no move to get back into his own car, she asked, "Why are you still standing there?"

"Because I'm waiting for you to get into your car so I can follow you home," he said simply.

"Follow me home?" she repeated incredulously. Her heart rate accelerated again in hushed anticipation. "Why would you do that?"

Did she think he was an idiot? "Because if I don't, you're going to turn around and go upstairs—and probably work through the night." He noticed that she didn't even try to deny it. Maybe he was finally making headway. "I was serious before—you're not going to do me or the task force any good working beyond the point of exhaustion. Now get in your car and drive home," he ordered. "Before I hog-tie you and drive you there myself."

"Fine," she snapped. He was right, but she definitely didn't like admitting it. She'd never liked being told what to do.

The streets were empty. She drove home in record time. When she reached her house, she half expected Declan to get out of his car and march her inside.

But he remained in his vehicle. When she didn't go to her front door immediately, Declan rolled down his window and gestured toward her door. "Go on," he urged. "Go inside."

Blowing out an exasperated breath, Charley opened her front door and went in.

When she came out again five minutes later, Declan was still parked in the same place, watching her.

"Are you planning to stay out here all night?" she called out to him, annoyed that he'd taken it upon himself to watch her.

"If I have to, yes," he answered without hesitation. "It all depends on you."

Charley realized that the exasperating detective with the lethal mouth meant it and if he did, then *he* would be the exhausted one tomorrow. God forbid they were called out for another victim. With only half his brain functioning, Declan would become a walking target. And if anything happened to him as a result of his compromised state, it would be her fault.

That wasn't anything that she was prepared to live with.

"Okay, okay, I'll go in and stay in," Charley shouted. Turning on her heel, she walked inside and slammed the door in her wake. Hard.

Declan remained parked at her curb for close to half an hour longer, during which time he watched her shut all the lights on the ground floor except for the one directly by the front door. Eventually, he decided that she had stopped being stubborn and had gone to bed.

Stifling a yawn, he started up his car and then drove home. It was late, but that didn't cause a problem. He had always had the ability to fall asleep instantly and tonight was no exception.

He was practically sound asleep the moment he walked in the front door.

Charley was back on the job almost at the crack of dawn. She came into the office, somewhat rested and ready to take a second or a third look if need be at the files, looking for that one slender clue that had been overlooked before. The clue that just might crack the case.

It continued to elude her.

Added to that, in the final analysis, she hadn't gotten all that much sleep despite the fact that Declan had forced her to go home. Ironically, he was the one who was the cause of her sleeplessness.

Every time she closed her eyes and began to drift off, she found herself reliving those few moments in the parking lot. Those few moments that at the time felt as if they were going to go on forever and had, for all intents and purposes, redefined her sense of reality.

When Declan came into the department just before eight o'clock, she was determined to act as if nothing had happened between them last night. She knew via rumors and her own observations, that Declan was accustomed to having women throw themselves at him. Once they'd been with him, to a woman they all acted as if all they wanted was to be with him again.

Permanently.

She was *not* about to join that club or be viewed, God forbid, as one of his "groupies." Yes, the man was a fantastic kisser and yes, she was exceedingly attracted to him, but that was a road that led nowhere and she knew it. She had a job to do, a killer to catch and a promise to keep.

She absolutely refused to get sidetracked.

Declan slid into his chair, depositing one of the large containers of coffee he was carrying on his desk. The other he pushed onto hers as if he'd been doing that all along instead of just this morning.

Was that a peace offering? she wondered. Or was that his way of saying that he felt like he owned her?

The latter was a crazy thought but ever since last night in the parking lot, her brain wasn't exactly thinking all that clearly. Black was white, up was down and everything in between was possible.

For now, she nodded toward the tall, covered container on her desk. "What's that?" she asked.

"Coffee," he told her absently, leaning back in his seat, his boots crossed before him and resting comfortably on another chair. "Why?" he asked. "What do you usually get in coffee containers?"

She didn't answer his question, saying instead, "You didn't have to do this."

"Yeah, I know." He shrugged off her statement. "Just thought it might keep everyone sharp first thing in the morning."

Everyone? That was when she looked around

and realized that he had dropped off a large container of coffee on the rest of the task force members' desks, as well.

"Oh," she murmured, feeling rather dumb for the thoughts she'd just been entertaining.

Idiot, the man has not only been around the block, he's been around the galaxy, for heaven's sake. You're not only not the only fish in the sea, you're not even the only fish in the aquarium, so get your mind back where it actually might do some good, she upbraided herself.

"By the way, what are you doing for breakfast tomorrow?" Declan asked after a beat. His attempt at nonchalance failed miserably.

"Breakfast?" she echoed, looking up. Now what was he getting at? Was he trying to find out if she was eating the right foods?

"Yeah, you know, the meal you eat right after you get up in the morning."

What did that have to do with anything? Frustrated, Charley shrugged at his question. "I don't know. Eating, I guess. Why?"

She wasn't sure he even heard her answer. His didn't quite mesh with what she'd just said. "I'll swing by and pick you up around seven, then."

This was coming out of the blue. Exactly what was he getting at? "Pick me up and take me where?" she asked.

"To Uncle Andrew's house." His computer was

having trouble booting up. He typed in a few commands on his keypad to get the program to come around. "The man loves to cook and he loves to have family come by so he can feed them." This was word of mouth, the invitation coming via his father, Sean. "He didn't have time to throw together one of his usual killer parties so he's just gonna have a big breakfast—and when he says 'big' the man means huge."

"What does this have to do with me?" she asked him.

"Uncle Andrew didn't exactly spell it out," Declan explained. "He just told me to bring you." His best guess was that his father had told Andrew that they were handling the case and Andrew wanted to give her the once-over. What better time than when she was eating one of his meals? "He thought you might enjoy being around a family gathering." That much was true, but that, too, had come via his father.

He had a feeling that if the invitation came to her thirdhand, she'd turn it down faster than she could draw a breath. Though he couldn't exactly say why, he found himself wanting her to be part of the wild circus that was his extended family.

She stared at Declan. The man he was talking about, Andrew Cavanaugh, had ceased being chief of police before she came onto the force. From what she'd heard, he'd retired early to raise his five children after his wife went missing and was presumed dead. Andrew never gave up hope that she was alive and eventually, his faith had paid off. Charley had the utmost respect for a man like that. But that still didn't begin to answer any of her basic questions.

"He doesn't even know me," she protested. So why would he want her there if he didn't know her?

"Uncle Andrew knows everyone," Declan assured her. In that, Andrew was very much like his younger brother, Brian. Both men seemed to have an eerie radar going for them when it came to the people working in the police department. "You don't want to insult the man by turning down an invitation—do you? And FYI, he really is a fantastic chef. The food is to die for—no pun intended."

She had no idea what to make of it or of the invitation she'd just been tendered. But Declan was right. She'd make no points in her present career if she turned down the former chief of police.

"Fine, I'll come," she told him. She made no attempt to hide the fact that she was more than a little bewildered.

A part of Charley felt like digging in her heels despite the fact that she was on the sidewalk and digging in would accomplish nothing, it would only be symbolic.

Doing her best to still the butterflies in her stomach, she tried to appear calm as she looked at Declan. "Are you sure this is all right?"

He could see how this sort of initial meeting might cause some anxiety, but he also knew the people she was meeting and they would all go the extra mile to put her at ease.

He knew that they certainly had when it had been his immediate family's turn. Granted, before his father's connection to the Cavanaugh family had come to light, he and his siblings had all been aware of at least some if not all of the various members of the impressive law-enforcement family. How could you be part of the Aurora P.D. and not be? But it still came under the heading of one of life's more pleasant shocks to discover that they were all actually blood relatives and he could personally attest that they were all—to a person—incredibly easy to get to know.

Rather than be standoffish the way some families might be, holding the "new guys" suspect, the established branches of the Cavanaugh clan welcomed them all with open arms. And he knew in his gut that although Charley wasn't a blood relative in the absolute sense, she was part of the police force that embraced them all.

Declan smiled to himself, thinking that there were times when, looking out on a gathering of Cavanaughs, depending if you were looking at the men or the women, you were looking at either a field of dark flowers or golden ones. He supposed that to an outsider, a lot of them tended to look alike. It was only once you got to know them that the things that set them apart, the subtle nuances, became apparent.

"Very sure," Declan replied.

"And the chief really won't mind my barging in?" Charley asked, allowing her uncertainty to surface. She could still turn around and go back, and right about now, that sounded like a pretty good idea.

Declan laughed at her choice of words. "You're not 'barging.' If anything, you're being dragged," he pointed out. "All that's missing is the kicking and screaming part." Amusement lit his eyes as well as his face.

They were at the front door and he was about to ring the bell, but Charley was growing more reluctant by the microsecond. "Look, maybe some other time would be better—" she began, trying her best to beg off.

"Now is always the best time," the tall man with the kind eyes said. Andrew Cavanaugh had opened the front door in time to hear the young woman beside his nephew trying to come up with an excuse to turn tail and run. "Besides, we're having breakfast, not human sacrifice. That's next Friday." And then he added, in case there was some tiny doubt in the young detective's mind, "I'm kidding."

"I know that," Charley said, raising her chin slightly in an automatic defensive move.

Noting the movement, Andrew didn't bother hiding his widening smile. Several of his nieces, not to mention his oldest daughter, did that when they were resorting to a show of bravado. This one was going to fit right in, he thought.

Putting his large hand out, he waited until she slipped hers into it. "Charley, right?" The question was a formality since he already knew who she was. He was the one who'd told Declan to bring her. He saw a glimmer of surprise in her eyes before she banked it down. "There're no secrets in the police force and definitely not in our family. I'm Andrew, by the way," he introduced himself, though it obviously wasn't necessary, adding, "You can call me Andrew or Chief. Call me 'Andy' and your breakfast will be cold," he quipped.

"Yes, sir, I mean—"

The smile turned into a grin. "Declan, find your partner a seat before she has a heart attack. And tell her I'm harmless," he threw in as he closed the door behind the duo.

"He *is* harmless, you know," Declan told her as he ushered her to the dining area where the rest of the family members who'd dropped by for breakfast were already seated. "Unless he's defending one of his own—then he's kind of scary," Declan added.

She'd never seen so much food in one place before. Appetizing-looking food, aromatic food that coaxed saliva glands into a state of anticipatory attention at lightning speed. Piled high on the extraordinary long table were breakfast crepes, some stuffed with blueberries, strawberries and tiny bits of pineapples, others with eggs, cheese and bits of fried ham. Other serving platters offered scrambled eggs, home fries, sausages, Canadian bacon and a host of other things that she didn't immediately recognized but that her palate wanted to be on a first-name basis with as soon as possible.

She took in the scene and was more than a little awestruck. This was Declan's family? "It looks like a town hall meeting," she whispered to Declan, standing just within the threshold. "They're all here for breakfast?" she marveled.

"Uncle Andrew makes the best everything," Declan stated matter-of-factly.

She thought of her own life, of how hard it had been at times for Matt just to feed the two of them. These people constituted a crowd. "How can he afford to feed everyone like this?"

"Well, there's not always this many people showing up, and we all make contributions to the groceries that're used," Declan said. "He's got a walk-in refrigerator in the garage as well as the biggest pantry I've ever seen. Any other questions?" he asked.

Still somewhat stunned, Charley shook her head. "No."

"Okay, then let's go in and sit down like he suggested. You don't want to insult the man, do you?" Declan deadpanned.

Was that what it looked like she was doing? "Oh, God, no."

Declan laughed. "Take it light, Charley. I'm just pulling your leg. Uncle Andrew doesn't insult easily, he just wants you to be at ease. The man loves to have his family around and he loves to cook. It's really all that simple," he told her.

"But I'm not—" she began.

He knew exactly what she was going to say. Something that about a third of the people there had said at one time or another. "You're a cop, so yeah, you are," he assured her. "Now relax and enjoy yourself."

"There're a couple of seats right over there," Callie, Andrew's oldest daughter, called out, pointing to two empty chairs on the far right of the extra-long dining room table. "If you two want to sit closer to the kitchen, I'm sure Shaw and Moira won't mind trading seats with you," she said, volunteering her older brother and his wife.

Charley looked toward the couple who'd just been pointed out to her. For a second, as recognition teased her brain, she stared at the man's wife. And then her mouth dropped open.

"You're Moira McCormick," she realized.

"Moira McCormick-Cavanaugh," the woman

corrected with a wide smile. "I'm semiretired now," she told Charley. "But I have my career to thank for bringing Shaw into my life."

Charley didn't quite understand, but she didn't want to pry. She was a guest here, not an investigative reporter.

"She came here to do research for a part and convinced Uncle Brian to have Shaw take her on a ride-along," Callie explained, then grinned. "They've been riding along with each other ever since."

"Good thing he didn't put her in Rayne's car," Troy, one of Brian's sons, quipped about Andrew's youngest daughter. "Moira would have gone running for the hills instead—right after her hair turned white."

"Don't listen to them," Rayne told her. "I don't drive that fast."

"Doesn't drive that fast?" Jared, another one of Brian's sons hooted. "NASCAR drivers send her fan letters. She's their official pinup girl."

Beginning to relax, Charley turned to her partner and asked, "Is it always like this?"

"No," he told her seriously. "It's usually rowdier. I think they're on their best behavior because you're here."

"You wouldn't know 'best behavior' if it bit you," Bridget, one of Declan's sisters, informed him.

In total, there were only a little less than a third of the Cavanaughs present, along with their spouses and assorted children, and even *that*, Charley discovered, amounted to almost twenty people. She found herself barely aware of what she was eating and very aware of who she was eating it with.

It made her a little envious of these people she had gotten to almost instantly know. She wondered if they knew how lucky they were. Yes, it was more than a bit noisy and probably pretty crowded when more of them showed up, but the feeling of camaraderie, of genuine affection, not to mention love, was something that even a stranger could easily detect. And that, she thought, was priceless in any person's book.

The hours seemed to feed into one another seamlessly from the moment she walked into the office. So much so that she didn't know when one ended and the next began.

Her breakfast with Declan and the Cavanaugh family at Andrew Cavanaugh's home the other morning had gone more than well. Declan's family, she discovered, effortlessly evaporated any feelings of awkwardness she'd harbored before walking into Andrew's house.

Matt would have really liked them, she'd thought. The almost impromptu occasion had made her more determined than ever to catch the shooter who had robbed her of her brother.

Because she and the rest of the task force had

seemingly hit a dead end, they had started from scratch, widening their circle to include cases that all three policemen had been involved in.

None overlapped. Even so, she was convinced that there had to be some kind of connection they were missing. She just hadn't made it yet.

Determined to solve Matt's murder and the murder of the other officers, Charley came in early, stayed late and danced with frustration because despite the effort, she was getting nowhere.

But at least there had been no new reports of victims and she took solace in that. Even so, she felt as if they were all on borrowed time.

The only time she'd stepped away from her desk the entire day was to take a ride to the funeral home that Declan had told her about. Though her bank account was fairly low, she needed to make arrangements for Matt's burial. The M.E. called her that morning to tell her that she was finally free to claim Matt's body at any time. Because she was pressed for time due to the current investigation, the medical examiner told her that he would keep Matt's body where it was until such time as she made her arrangements.

She hated thinking of Matt locked away in a drawer, a toe tag serving as his prime piece of cover. Taking out the name and number she'd hastily scribbled down, she called the funeral parlor and asked them to pick Matt up, then told the man she would be in at noon to make the arrangements.

When noon came, she told Declan she had an errand to run and left before he could say anything.

The funeral director, Malcolm Avery, was a soft-spoken man who could have easily blended in anywhere without being noticed. The sum of money he quoted, when pressed, for a typical funeral took her breath away. The amount didn't seem real.

She had always lived rather frugally, but there still wasn't enough money set aside to take care of the funeral arrangements she wanted for Matt, at least not all at once.

There was no way around this. Though the sum was high, she didn't want to scrimp, not on this, not for Matt. He deserved the best she could give him.

Though it killed her to ask, Charley knew she had no choice.

"Do you have a payment plan?" she asked the director. "I could make regular payments every month until the bill is paid off—" she began, hating the awkward feeling she was experiencing. This felt almost like begging, despite the fact that she had every intention of paying for the funeral arrangements.

The funeral director looked at her, confusion evident on his brow. "Detective Randolph, I'm afraid I'm a bit puzzled. There's nothing to pay off."

Okay, that made two of them who were confused. She looked at the director blankly. He'd just told her how much the arrangements like the one she'd suggested cost. How could that just disappear the next moment?

"Excuse me?"

"The arrangements have all been paid for. Your loved one is to have our exclusive deluxe package," the man told her gently. "I know that sounds extremely commercial," he admitted, referring to the wording he'd just used, "but what it means is that there was no expense spared."

This wasn't making any sense. She held up her hand, stopping him. "Wait, wait, there has to be some mistake," she said. "These arrangements are for Sergeant Matthew Holt—"

"Yes, I know," the funeral director confirmed. "That's what I have written down. All expenses are taken care of."

"By whom?" Charley asked.

The director shook his head, looking somewhat apologetic. "I'm not at liberty to say," he told her sympathetically.

Had the police union paid for Matt's funeral? But then, wouldn't she have been notified? This wasn't making any sense. She hadn't approached anyone for help with the finances; why would someone step up for her?

"Can you at least tell me if it was an individual or the police union?" she asked the director.

He looked uncomfortable. "All I can say is that the gentleman who paid for the arrangements didn't want you to have to worry about anything."

Well, that answered her question if it was the union that had taken it upon itself to bury her brother. They hadn't. Which meant—she had a hunch who actually might have come to her rescue.

At least, these were the only dots she had to try to connect.

She went back to the police station—and Declan.

Chapter 14

Declan turned from his computer the moment Charley walked into the squad room. He couldn't even say how he knew she was there, he just did.

"You get everything taken care of?" he asked Charley.

Something in the way he asked had her looking at Declan for a long moment. He was the one who'd paid for Matt's funeral, she was willing to bet her life on it. There was obviously more to this man than she had ever thought. Back when they were both attending the academy, although she was secretly attracted to him, to his electric demeanor, she'd still written him off as someone who, at least in his personal life, was only interested in having a good time. He didn't act like he possessed a serious, responsible bone in his body.

If that *had* been Declan back then, it certainly wasn't the Declan she was interacting with these past few days.

"Apparently," she finally replied.

Declan raised one eyebrow. "What's that supposed to mean?"

"It means that in this particular case, you would know just as much as I do whether or not everything was taken care of."

For a minute, she debated leaving it at that. But she couldn't. Though her pride had urged her to refuse what he had covertly done, she knew that this wasn't a time for pride, it was a time for gratitude. He'd done it anonymously and thus with the best of intentions.

Their eyes met and held for another very long moment before she said, "It was you, wasn't it?"

"It was me, what?" he asked innocently, his expression giving away nothing.

She didn't want to play games. And she was not about to accept charity—from anyone.

"You know damn well what I'm talking about. Look, I can pay my own way," she said, then added more quietly, "Just not completely at the moment." He was still acting as if he didn't know what she was talking about, but she plowed ahead. "I'll make the same arrangement with you I was going to make with the funeral home. I'll pay you back in equal installments until you have the full amount back—with interest."

Declan's expression remained unchanged. "Although I'd love some extra money, I have no idea what you're talking about."

"You didn't pay for Matt's funeral." It was more of an accusation than a question.

He merely shook his head. "Nope."

He appeared unshakable, but Charley didn't believe him. "You swear?"

Declan shrugged, turning his chair back around so that he faced his computer screen. "I swear."

Grabbing the chair's arms, Charley forced it back around so that he was facing her again. She wanted the truth and she only knew one way to get at it.

"On your mother's grave," she pressed, thinking that invoking the memory of his mother might be the one thing that would make him think twice about covering up his good deed with a lie. "You swear you didn't do it on your mother's grave," she repeated.

She had him.

Declan sighed. "What's the big deal? Instead of wasting my money on some vacation I won't remember three days after it's over, I'm using it to help bury a good cop. To me that's a good investment."

"It's not an investment, it's a loan and I'm paying you back," she insisted.

She had enough to contend with right now, he didn't want her facing monetary woes, as well. "You don't have to."

"Yeah," Charley contradicted, "I do."

He shrugged again. She was immovable and he was not about to push it. "Whatever makes you happy," he told her. "Funeral's tomorrow?" It was a calculated guess on his part.

Charley nodded. In having it so soon, she was forgoing the traditional three-day viewing period. But as her last act of protection, she was going to keep prying eyes away from her brother. She knew he would have wanted it that way if he could have been able to have a say in the matter. He was, at bottom, a private person.

"What time?" Declan asked.

"Sunset," she answered. "It was Matt's favorite time of day. I never knew why. Now I can't ask him."

Declan offered her his thoughts on the matter. "Probably because the day was over and everything was winding down."

Sounded as good as any theory, she supposed, but before she could express her thoughts on Declan's assessment, one of the other three detectives, Bobby Yu, swung around in his chair, away from his desk.

Terminating the phone call that had just come in on his line, Bobby announced, "Looks like we're up, boys and girls." He looked at Declan. "Dispatch said your line's not working, so she called the closest phone to yours, which for some reason turned out to be mine." Bobby shrugged, dismissing the subject since that wasn't the important part. "Homeless guy going through a Dumpster behind a local restaurant found a dead man instead of dinner."

"A cop?" Declan asked.

"Is there any other kind lately?" Bobby answered grimly.

"And they found him in a Dumpster?" That didn't sound right, Declan thought, on his feet and checking his service revolver before holstering it. That sounded more like the killer was trying to hide the body after he'd killed him and he had left the others where they could easily be found.

"Not *in* the Dumpster," Bobby corrected. "Next to it. The officer had one shot to the chest, just like all the others."

"And a note?" Charley asked grimly. "Was there a note stapled to his chest?"

"Dispatch didn't say," Bobby told her. "Doesn't mean there wasn't one."

"The Santa Anas have been acting up," Detective Callaghan reminded them, referring to the winds that blew in from the desert around this time of year. They were usually hot, intolerable and rather strong. "If the note wasn't really secured, it could have blown away."

"As long as we find staple marks on his chest, that should be enough to link him to the same killer," Declan theorized. "You got the address?" he asked Bobby. Rather than answer, the other detective held up a piece of paper that he had written on. "Great. Okay, let's roll," he told his team.

But as Charley began to get up, he put his hand on her shoulder and physically stopped her. "Why don't you stay and man the phones, call us if something else comes up."

There was no way she was going to sit here, playing nursemaid to a landline. "You can tell the administrative assistant to do that," Charley said, her tone making it very clear that the only way he could get her to stay behind was if he physically tied her to her chair—and maybe not even then.

Declan relented. "Yeah, I suppose I can."

"And stop trying to shield me," she ordered him. "You're not going to succeed."

There was succeed, and then there was *succeed*. The important part was that she understood she wasn't alone in this, didn't have to go through it alone.

"Someone has to try," he told her matter of factly as they hurried out.

She didn't want his answer to matter to her. But it did.

* * *

The latest victim was a police officer just coming off duty. As with the other murder victims, there were no apparent signs of struggle. No bruised knuckles, no defensive wounds. The officer, Juan Sierra, hadn't gone down fighting.

There was, however, a look of complete surprise frozen on his face.

"Not horror, just surprise," Charley noted, studying the man's expression closely. "Like he couldn't believe what he was seeing." She glanced up at Declan. "What do you think that means?"

"That whoever shot him didn't look threatening until Sierra saw the gun being pointed at him. What was happening probably didn't even register until after he went down." Pity and compassion mixed with frustrated anger filtered across his face. "What's this guy trying to do, eliminate the force, one officer at a time?" There had to be a connection between these men that they were missing. There *had* to be. "There's got to be some kind of reason, no matter how screwed up, that he's doing this."

"Yeah, but what?" Charley asked, sharing his frustration. They were almost at the end of their lists of men—and the handful of women—who had either washed out, were turned away because they failed their psych evaluations, or had been terminated because of some sort of "unbecoming conduct" that rendered them unfit for duty in the police department's eyes.

"Sooner or later, he's going to trip up," Sanchez said hopefully. "He's *got* to."

"Yeah, but how many more cops are we going to lose before that happens?" Charley asked. Even one more was one too many.

Declan turned toward one of the members of the CSI unit who had come out to collect evidence. Lisa Sullivan was taking photograph after photograph, the high-end digital camera in her hand making continuous whirling noises as she snapped away.

He moved into her line of vision, causing her to stop snapping and look up. Only then did Declan say, "I want a copy of every photo you've taken from Sergeant Holt through this one—Officer Sierra. Send them to my computer," he instructed.

"I'll send them as soon as I get back to the lab," the woman promised, then, curious, asked, "Think we missed something that's out in plain sight?"

"That's what I'm hoping," Declan told her honestly as he turned back to his own part in the investigation.

For the next hour, he and Charley questioned the restaurant employees, but as with all the other crime scenes, no one recalled hearing or seeing anything out of the ordinary.

Unlike the other three murders, this murder had

taken place with two security cameras in close proximity, although neither was placed to face the alley.

Hoping that one of the cameras might have caught *something,* Declan commandeered the surveillance tapes for that day, promising to return them once they were finished reviewing them.

"What are you hoping to see?" Charley asked once they were back in the squad room.

"I don't know," he confessed. "Something that might just lead us down the right trail for a change." It was a case of knowing it once he saw it, not before.

She supposed, in a desperate way, that made sense. She took a closer glance at Declan. "You look as beat as I feel," she told him. "Maybe you should knock it off for the night."

Declan laughed, shaking his head in disbelief. How had the tables turned? "Now *you're* mothering *me?*"

"Was that what you were doing the other night in the parking lot?" she asked, amusement entering her eyes. "Mothering me?"

"That wasn't the first word that came to mind," he admitted.

Everything about that small interlude had lingered on his mind, like the lyrics of a song that was stuck in his head and refused to fade away.

She smiled at him then. Beyond tired and every

bit as frustrated as she knew he was, Charley still managed to laugh—or maybe she laughed because she was beyond tired and her defenses at this point were pretty close to nonexistent.

"Me neither," she agreed.

"Make you a deal," he said, glancing toward the door and the hallway just beyond. "I'll go home if you do."

She looked at the disk in her hand that she was getting ready to watch. Most likely, in her present state, she was fairly certain that it would put her right to sleep within a quarter of an hour if not sooner.

"Okay," she agreed. "Fresh eyes might be better at that. I'll go through the security tapes tomorrow."

But the next day was the funeral, an event she had managed to temporarily block from her mind until she woke up that morning.

As much as she wanted to be able to finally find something that would help lead her to Matt's killer, she needed to be at his funeral more. Needed to say one final goodbye.

Getting ready for the church service was harder than she thought.

Accustomed to rushing around at home when she was getting ready to go to work, she found this time that someone had drained the blood from her veins and substituted molasses. No matter how Charley tried, her sense of urgency just refused to kick in.

She knew it was because she really didn't want to go to the ceremony, didn't want to hear the priest say words over the coffin that was to be her brother's final resting place. Didn't want to see that "resting place" lowered into the ground.

Didn't really want to say goodbye, even though it was just a formality. Her brother was already gone.

Fighting off tears, she didn't hear the doorbell at first. At what point the ringing actually registered with her brain, she didn't know, but her first reaction to the sound was to ignore it.

She wasn't expecting anyone.

And then she remembered that she was.

Taking a deep breath, she walked over to the front door and opened it.

Declan was standing there, wearing a dark suit and looking far more subdued than she remembered ever seeing him.

He looked good in a suit, she thought absently, then felt bad having a thought like that on the day she was burying Matt.

"You really don't have to come," she told Declan. Charley hated that he felt somehow obligated to prop her up, even if it was the very blackest time in her life.

She looked fragile, he noted. Like a porcelain doll that gave the impression it would crack if the slightest pressure was applied to it. He caught himself wanting to scoop her up into his arms and keep her safe. No one should have to go through what she was going through.

He wasn't about to go anywhere but with her. Whether she was willing to admit it or not, she needed him.

"Want me to pull rank?" he asked.

The question coaxed a smile out of her. Leave it to him to ask that. "No," she answered.

"Good, then let's go."

Rather than just walk out beside her, Declan presented his arm to her. It was a precautionary step because she gave the impression that she just might sink to the ground at any moment.

"Just so you know, I'm driving," he informed her. His tone left no room for dissent or argument. Nor did she offer any.

Charley suddenly felt completely, utterly drained. Though she would have never admitted it out loud, she was silently grateful that Declan had taken it upon himself to take charge.

Charley really wasn't expecting anyone to attend the funeral. Matt got along well with the people he worked with, but he'd always kept his professional life and his private life separated. He didn't get together with his friends from work once he walked out of the precinct at night.

Moreover, because of this killer, there were a number of other funerals to go to. That was why she was surprised when the church not only filled up with people coming to pay their last respects, but by the time the ceremony started, there was standing room only.

A number of people, including the chief of detectives, all came up to the pulpit to share a few words, in some cases a few stories about the deceased, with the mourners.

Charley found herself fighting tears throughout the ceremony and then again at the cemetery. A lot of the faces she recognized as people she'd met at Andrew Cavanaugh's house when she'd gone with Declan for breakfast.

She was at a loss for words.

When the service at the grave site was over, she became aware of the fact that Declan was watching over her.

When had he put his arm protectively around her? She couldn't remember.

"Ready?" he asked.

She knew what he was asking. If she was ready to leave. He gave her the impression that he was prepared to stay as long as she needed him to.

Charley nodded her head. "Ready." He began to usher her toward his car. She looked around her at all the people who had turned out for her brother. Her heart felt close to bursting.

"I should have prepared something," she said with regret. "I should have put together a reception. I just didn't think there'd be so many people coming to the service."

Declan smiled at her. "It's all taken care of," he said.

She didn't understand. "What's all taken care of?" she asked him.

"Uncle Andrew invited everyone who attended the service to come over to his house. He's having the reception there."

She was utterly stunned. The man didn't know her, except for that one time. Why had he taken it upon himself to go out of his way like this? Somehow or another, this had to be Declan's doing, she realized.

"I don't know what to say," she told him.

"Say you'll come."

Startled, Charley turned around to see who had said that. She found herself looking up at the kind, crystal-blue eyes of the man who everyone regarded as the family patriarch despite Shamus's return from Florida and his defunct retirement.

She realized that the former chief of police was waiting for an answer.

"I'll come," Charley replied.

Andrew smiled at her, nodding his approval. He knew how hard this was for her. He'd lost a brother

in the line of duty and thought he'd lost a wife—
though he never gave up looking for her.

"Good girl," he said. "I'll see you at the house."
Picking up his pace, he got into a long black sedan
driven by his brother Sean.

A little shell-shocked, Charley shook her head
in complete amazement. "You Cavanaughs do take
over," she said to Declan.

"Sometimes that turns out to be a good thing,"
he said gently. He slipped his arm through hers as
he brought her over to his vehicle.

"Yes," she replied, thinking how much she ap-
preciated the genuine warmth she'd just seen dem-
onstrated by Declan's uncle Andrew. "I know."

Chapter 15

The moment Charley walked into Andrew's house, the rest of the Cavanaughs embraced her as if she were one of them.

And, technically, she was.

She was a police detective, which, to the members of the law-enforcement family, easily made her one of their own. She was one of the people who laid her life on the line every day and that sort of thing brought with it a sense of kinship that superseded everything else. That meant that Matt had been one of them as well and they were honoring him as such.

And comforting her.

There could have been no better way to get past any normal barriers that Charley might have had. Barriers that kept her safe, but at the same time, served to isolate her.

If they were aware of the barrier, Andrew and the others gave no indication. Instead, they reached out to her with compassion and sympathy as if there was nothing in the way, nothing to stop them.

They wouldn't allow it.

It was like that from the first moment they had gathered around her at the church until the end of the evening, when Andrew finally walked her and Declan to the door of his home, sending them on their way with good wishes and instructions to return the next weekend for a large family gathering he had planned.

Charley left Andrew's house a little overwhelmed—and smiling. Being around the family had helped her deal with her pain and she was grateful to them. And to Declan for his part in all this.

In sharp contrast to the constant din of voices dovetailing into one another, there was silence as they walked to his car.

That same silence accompanied them for part of the ride back to her house. Declan felt she might need a little quiet time to process everything, so he waited until she felt like talking.

"You're lucky," she said softly after several minutes had passed.

"How's that?" he asked. Her remark could have been taken in half a dozen different ways and he waited for her to elaborate before making any kind of a comment.

"Having a family like that," she said. "You're never alone."

He inclined his head, knowing she was right. There was always someone to back him up, someone to rely on. Someone to turn to if he needed guidance in some undertaking.

"To be honest, there have been times when I would have given anything to be left alone, to have some peace and quiet," he said.

"It's highly overrated," she told him.

He slanted a look in her direction. She was putting on a tough exterior, but she still made him think of a wounded bird. "You know, you don't have to come in tomorrow," he pointed out. "You're entitled to some bereavement time. Why don't you take a few days off?"

That was the last thing she wanted.

"And do what?" she asked. "Knock around my house—or Matt's—and think?" Matt had left his house to her, but it was going to be a while before she could bring herself to go through it. "I'll go crazy before the day's over. No, I need to keep busy, to be doing something to find and catch that sick bastard who did this. I'm coming in," she decided.

He nodded as he turned down her street. He had

to make the offer, but to be honest, he expected her to say that.

"I'd probably do the same thing in your place," he admitted.

Declan pulled up in front of her house. Rather than keep the car running as he waited for her to get out, he turned the engine off and got out. Rounding the hood of his vehicle, he came around to her side. She'd already opened the door, but he took her hand and helped her out. For once, she let him.

"I *can* find my own front door," she told him with a hint of a smile.

"Humor me," Declan muttered as he walked with her. And then he grew serious. "If you need anything, *anything* at all, you know you can call me, right?"

Charley turned from the door she'd just unlocked and nodded. "Yes," she said quietly, "I know."

Raising her eyes to his, she began to search for the words to thank him for everything. Most of all, for letting her continue with the investigation despite the fact that he'd found out that Matt was her brother. She wanted, too, to thank him for just being there.

For some reason, the words just refused to materialize. Because Matt had taught her that action spoke louder than words, she rose up on her toes and brushed a kiss against his lips.

Just like the first time, a jolt of electricity accompanied the contact, zigzagging through her. Unlike the first time, the contact was not brief. Instead, the kiss, intense and filled with emotions as well as no small amount of vulnerability, gave birth to another kiss. And then another one, each longer and stronger than the last.

Charley didn't remember just exactly when her arms went around his neck, or when her body leaned, then pressed against his. She didn't remember feeling as if she'd lost her way because, suddenly, she'd found it, stumbling through a portal she hadn't even known was there.

A portal that took her from the world she knew, a world where everything was clearly, neatly defined and labeled, a world that was structured so that she could find her way around even in the dark, into a world that was comprised of emotions and passions and needs that flared to such a degree they would have consumed her had there not been something for her to gravitate toward.

Though she didn't remember the exact logistics—even as they were happening—one moment she was on her doorstep, the next she was inside her house, the door slammed shut, the rest of the world barred from entry, with only the two of them to populate this brave new world unfolding before her.

Damn, so much for the hope that the first time had been a fluke. If anything, it paled in comparison to the way he felt right now, completely wrapped up in this woman he was supposed to be partnered with.

There was a need eating away at him, taking out huge chunks at a time. Declan had no doubt that all of him would be gone soon, sacrificed to this burning desire he was experiencing. A burning desire to be with her, to make love with her.

To lose himself completely within her until he wasn't sure where he ended and she began.

Not that it mattered.

He'd always, always, even when it was his first time, had a clear head. He'd never been governed by his emotions, never been led around by his passions…before. Logic and common sense had always been his navigators. Now logic was nowhere to be found and all he knew was that he'd wind up burning down to a useless cinder if he couldn't have her.

And have her soon.

But this is wrong, something inside his head screamed. He was taking advantage of the moment, of her vulnerability. Never mind that she had started it by kissing him, he was at fault for not at least attempting to talk her out of it. He hadn't backed away and made her understand that it was the fear of being alone that was driving her this way. That was making her do what she was doing—connecting with him.

Lightly framing her face with his hands, Declan forced himself to pull back from her.

When he did, Charley appeared bewildered, as if she'd done something wrong to make him stop, but hadn't a clue as to what that one wrong thing was.

"You don't want to do this," Declan told her gently.

"No offense," Charley replied, her voice low, her body aching, "but you don't have a clue what I want."

He caught her hands as she was about to put them back around his neck. She might want this now, but what of tomorrow? Was she going to look back with an overwhelming sense of shame tomorrow?

"I don't want you doing something you'll regret in the morning."

"I'll only regret it if we stop right now," she said softly.

He felt her breath along his skin, felt her yearning pulsating and mingling with his own. Declan had always prided himself on being a strong man, but in this case, his strength had only gone so far and it was now in retreat.

He'd reached his limit. He didn't have it in him to hold her back or hold himself in check, any longer than he just had.

So when Charley brought her mouth back up to his, he didn't stop her.

He *couldn't* stop her. Because the second her mouth touched his, the explosive desire returned.

In triplicate.

Very quickly, the path from her front door up to her bedroom was littered with articles of clothing. Hers and his, mingling, overlapping.

For each piece that she took off him, Declan removed one from her, all while their lips were sealed to one another.

A flurry of movement, becoming faster and faster, marked their trail until somehow, almost defying gravity—certainly defying memory—they were in her bedroom, as naked as the day they were born, bathed in desire that took all inhibitions, all common sense away and replaced it with the anticipation of ecstasy that was impossible to contain.

For all his experience, Declan felt like a novice all over again, because he'd never been down this road, never felt desire causing every fiber of his being to vibrate the way that it did this minute. That final moment of passionate fulfillment shimmered before him like a tempting mirage in the desert, coaxing him to go on, seducing him.

Holding him prisoner as with each passing moment, he drew closer and closer to that last wild, gratifying moment that was still eluding him.

So this was what it was like. This was what it felt like to want someone, to *need* someone with every fiber of her body and soul. She'd thought these kinds of things were the stuff that wistful songs and fairy tales were made of. But in real life, she'd been certain that they didn't exist.

In real life, the mingling of two bodies, of *sex,* was just that: sex. Cold, hard and there.

Nothing magical about it.

But she'd been wrong.

Really wrong and she'd never been so happy to be wrong in her life.

Every inch of her felt as if it was in competition with itself. In competition for his touch, his caress, for the intoxicating feel of his lips along her skin. Every place that came in contact with some part of him arched against him, as if silently—and not so silently—begging for more.

Begging for those ever mounting peaks that kept forming within her, exploding even as they whispered promises of *more.*

He felt her climaxes and experienced them by proxy, growing more and more excited with each one that he felt vibrating through her body.

Charley made him wild with anticipation until he couldn't keep himself in check a second longer.

Enfolding her in his arms, Declan brought his body to hers, aligned himself with hers just so.

And then he entered.

Biting her lower lip, Charley smothered a cry of pleasure as she arched even more, her body silently inviting him to take what had been his from the very beginning.

Declan didn't remember when he began to move in sync with her, only that the rhythm increased almost from the beginning and she matched him, thrust for thrust, slowly, pleasurably driving him over the edge.

He held on to her as if she was his very lifeline, not to the world, but to paradise.

The anticipation grew, becoming ever stronger, until suddenly, it tightened around them and burst forth, sending out sky rockets and fireworks of unimaginable beauty, breadth and intensity.

Declan held on to it—and her—for all he was worth.

If he died this moment, that would be fine with him. Because he had *lived*.

Gradually, as the earth began to appear below him, he became aware of the pounding of Charley's heart. The pulsating sound was an echo of his own.

Other things came into focus—and along with them, his conscience.

For a few seconds—or was it minutes?—he just lay there, continuing to draw breath and nothing more. But he knew that he could only put off the inevitable for so long. After all, he couldn't play dead or pretend to be asleep indefinitely. Eventually, he was going to have to face her.

He might as well do it now.

He began formulating his apology slowly. "Did I hurt you?" he asked.

The words disappeared in her hair. He'd said

them against the top of her head and while she felt the vibration of his voice along her skull, she couldn't really make out the words.

Turning her head, moving it away from his lips, Charley asked, "What?"

"Did I hurt you?" Declan asked again, obviously concerned.

The question struck her as funny. She laughed softly at it. "I'd say the exact opposite." She turned her head so that it was resting against his chest. Her breath was burned into his chest with every word she said. "Why would you think that?" she asked. As far as she knew, she'd given no indication of being on the receiving end of pain.

"Because I just went ahead. I didn't give you a chance to say no." He was inching his way closer to an apology.

"You would have had a long wait," she told him with a smile.

Looking at him now, her smile grew wider. He was probably worried about what she was thinking now after what had happened between them. He had definitely rocked her world, but she knew that the odds of her doing the same to his were little to none. And now that the fun part was over, he was probably concerned about the possible consequences.

"Don't worry," she reassured him, "I'm not holding you to anything. I'm a big girl, Declan. This had no strings attached."

"Right. Good to know," he said, the words dribbling forth slowly from his lips.

But for the first time, Declan realized that he wanted strings.

"But you know, now that I think of it," Declan told her, "I never had a 'no strings' conversation with you."

"You didn't have to," she replied.

Though she had told herself that she was more than sated, something within her was all but pulling toward this man with the incredibly hard body again. Even now, her body was half resonating from what had just taken place and half tingling with anticipation of what was lying ahead.

"Oh?" Declan asked, his curiosity, as well as his body, aroused. "And why's that?"

"Because no man wants strings."

"My brothers did," he pointed out, finding himself reacting to her all over again. *Wanting* her all over again. "The other Cavanaugh men in the family did," he went on.

"The rookie at the Academy who drew women to him like a high-powered magnet didn't," she reminded him.

"The academy," he told her, his fingertips languidly moving along either side of her body, memorizing each contour, tantalizing them both, "is years in the past. And I'm not."

"If anything," she countered, arching her body

against his, every part of her being humming with yearning, "that rookie would be even more prone to keep moving from willing woman to willing woman."

"Guess again," he whispered against her mouth just before his lips covered hers.

It all sounded so pretty, so wonderful, but they were words he was saying, just words, Charley reminded herself. She had to remember that and not get too caught up in all this. As long as she was aware that this—all of this—was just temporary, she'd be all right.

At least, that was the plan.

Darkness slowly crept in and took possession of the room as the sun outside receded in the sky, moving on in its orbit.

The figure on the sofa didn't move, hardly breathed.

The person who had been immobile for the past half hour, thinking, continued to stare at the bulletin board that hung on the opposite wall. The bulletin board where covertly taken photographs had been hung.

Photographs of police officers, all of whom were carefully selected and marked for death.

The first four photographs each had a large red *X* drawn through them. These were the targets that had been eliminated.

Men who could no longer draw a breath.

Men who *shouldn't* have been able to draw breath for as long as they did.

But justice, long overdue, had been served in their cases. There was more justice to be handed out.

This was not the time for resting, for sitting and basking in past accomplishments. This was a time for action—because other targets were waiting to be taken out.

So many more targets.

And each and every one of them was guilty. Each and every one of the police officers on that bulletin board deserved to die.

Should have already died.

The shooter beat back the wave of mounting frustration. It would take patience. With patience everything was possible.

Rising from the sofa, the tall, previously inert figure seemed to come alive.

Moving with purpose, the shooter crossed the Spartan-looking living room and came to stand before the bulletin board.

"Which one of you will be next? Which will be the next one to die? Any volunteers?"

Different people required different plans and everything had to be timed, had to go down just so. There was no room for error.

The shooter wouldn't stand for it.

"Doesn't really matter which one of you will be next," the shooter finally said, an eerie laugh scratching the night air as it accompanied the words. "You're all going to be in the same place soon. You're all going to be dead."

Relishing the thought, the shooter's mouth curved into an icy smile of anticipation.

On his way home the next evening, Andrew Cavanaugh smiled to himself.

It had been a good, extremely productive and satisfying day.

It wasn't often that he patted himself on the back for something, but this definitely was one of those rare times. Through his efforts of relentless investigation, he'd not only discovered the missing branch of his family that his father had charged him with finding, he'd made contact with them. Not only that, but he made arrangements to have the entire bunch—and it *was* a bunch—come out to his place a week from next Saturday so that they could get acquainted with a lot of family that they hadn't even realized existed.

Who would have thought that the missing branch of the family was only a city away? And that those members were all, just as they were here, entrenched in law enforcement?

He didn't normally believe in coincidences, but this, certainly, was one.

It was a damn small world, he thought with a chuckle.

He was really tired, but at the same time, he was very pleased with himself.

He'd called Rose before he left and shared everything. She was as excited as he was. He'd ended the call by telling her that he was coming home tonight, but it might be late so she shouldn't wait up.

As if she'd listen to him, he thought with a soft laugh. The light of his life listened to him when she wanted to, did what she wanted the rest of the time.

It didn't matter. He was a hell of a lucky man and he knew it.

He—

His breath caught in his throat as he thought he made out something up ahead.

Damn, what *was* that?

He felt for his shirt pocket.

Where had he put his glasses? He should have worn them, but they made him feel old.

Hell, you are old, a voice in his head said.

Andrew squinted. He thought he saw something staggering up ahead in the road. Not wanting to take any chances, he swerved at the last minute to keep from hitting it.

As his car spun to the left, he struggled to regain control of it.

Andrew was so busy trying to steer into the spin,

he didn't see the person in the middle of the road raising a gun until it was too late.

The single, resounding shot went into his windshield, shattering it.

The last thing Andrew Cavanaugh was aware of was the windshield glass falling inside his vehicle like so many bits of fragmented snowflakes.

The pain in his chest consumed him, blotting out the entire world.

Chapter 16

The bent, ragged, homeless man who had appeared to have been so preoccupied with pawing through the overflowing trash cans that were lined up in the alley instantly came to attention at the first sound of tires squealing.

Eyes on the fishtailing white sedan in the middle of the deserted road, the undercover DEA agent heard the gunshot screaming through the night air and then saw the shooter walking toward the immobilized vehicle.

By then he stopped pretending to be a spectator and was sprinting toward the car and the victim he glimpsed inside it.

That was when the shooter realized there was someone else in the vicinity besides the driver who was presumably taken out. Swallowing a livid curse, the shooter dropped the note that was meant to be stapled to the newest victim's chest, turned around and ran back into the shadows, seeking the cover of night.

Intent on survival, the shooter didn't see the ragged man dragging the former chief of police from his car. Otherwise, risky or not, a second shot would have pierced the night air.

Just to be sure the deed was done.

The landline on her nightstand rang insistently, intruding into a hard-won slumber that had claimed Charley as well as the man sleeping beside her. What had begun as a one-time effort to comfort her had turned out to be something beyond that. Something with a little more breadth and substance than just a mutually enjoyed seduction.

After putting in a more than full day today, going through all the surveillance tapes they had confiscated, neither Charley nor he had any desire to say good-night. So Declan had come home with her. Again. And he had made love with her. Again.

Charley silently lectured herself not to expect this to turn into a regular pattern. She knew better than that. Thought she knew *him* better than that.

But while it was happening, she intended to enjoy every single second for as long as it continued.

Disoriented for less than a second, Declan, not Charley, sat up and reached for the phone, picking the receiver up by the third ring and placing it to his ear before his eyes were fully focused on anything.

And when they were, it was on the woman in bed beside him. Charley had turned out to be one hell of a wild woman in bed—who knew?

"Cavanaugh," he said automatically, momentarily forgetting that it was Charley's phone, not his, that he had answered.

"Declan?" the deep male voice asked uncertainly.

The voice registered at the same time that a feeling of dark foreboding took hold. Something was off.

"Shane? What are you doing, calling at this hour?" And why was his brother calling Charley?

Charley sat up, watching Declan, feeling the same sense of restless, formless fear that he was dealing with. Something was wrong. She could feel it in her gut.

"It's Andrew," his brother said grimly. "He's been shot."

Declan felt his stomach drop down to his toes. "When?" he asked. "How? Is it serious?" He fired the questions rapidly as he looked around the room, trying to remember where his clothes were.

"We don't know yet. He's in surgery. Aurora General," Shane replied.

"I'll be there as soon as I can," Declan said. Shane was still talking as he dropped the receiver back into the cradle.

"What's happening?" Charley asked.

Declan was already hurrying into the clothes he'd hastily shed last night, when the only thing that mattered at the time was making love with Charley again, of revisiting the incredible exhilarating feeling being with her generated.

Now that seemed like a lifetime ago.

"Someone shot Andrew," he told her. "Shane said he's in surgery. I don't know any more than that." But he intended to find out.

Charley's feet hit the ground as she grabbed for the first clothes that were handy. She was dressed half a beat after he was. She could be exceptionally quick when the need called for it.

"I'll drive," she said.

He didn't argue. There was no time for that.

They made it to the hospital in what amounted to record time. There was very little traffic on the road and Charley had flown through the yellow lights as well as the green ones.

When they reached the hospital's parking lot, it looked as if it was the middle of the day instead of the middle of the night. The lot right behind the

E.R. entrance, as well as the one adjacent to it, was crammed with vehicles. Vapors of heat still hovered over the hooded engines of a large portion of them.

Parking as best she could, she and Declan hurried out of her vintage vehicle and hurried to the E.R.'s automatic doors.

There was no need to say anything to the receptionist on duty. The second they entered, the woman in the blue livery pointed to the doors on her left that led down the hallway.

"Can't miss it," she assured them as she continued typing something into her data program.

The second they went through the swinging doors, Declan saw what the woman meant. It looked like another one of Andrew's get-togethers, except that everyone there seemed grim.

A very harried-looking nurse was trying to find a way to contain the ever-growing crowd. This wasn't her first time at the rodeo.

"Please, people, find waiting rooms to disperse into. You'll be notified the second the chief is out of surgery. I promise."

No one made a move, not wanting to be the last to receive any sort of word, good or bad, all waiting for someone else to step aside.

Failing to get anyone to leave, the fifteen-year nursing veteran sighed, shaking her head. "You people need to get your own hospital," she muttered under her breath, retreating into one of the side rooms that lined the hallway.

Declan saw his father and Rose, Andrew's wife, at the same time. Undecided for a moment who to speak to, he approached his father. He didn't want to say anything that might possibly upset the chief's wife any more than she already had to be.

"Dad?" Declan said the second he and Charley were within hearing range. "How is he?"

Sean shook his head. "They won't tell us. All they said was that he was still breathing."

Well, at least that was good, Charley thought. "What happened?" she asked.

"We think the cop killer ambushed him," Sean answered grimly. He motioned toward someone to his left to come forward. "I'll let the guy who saved him give you the details."

Declan and she turned in unison to look at the man Sean was referring to.

Disheveled, with matted hair and a week's growth, the aromatic man who stepped forward was the kind who faded into the background of any urban street. Here, amid the Cavanaugh family, he stood out like the proverbial sore thumb, looking every inch the homeless man he'd been portraying for the past six months.

Only the intelligent, alert eyes gave up the persona he was projecting.

"You're undercover?" Declan guessed.

The other man grinned, shaking his head. "It's not supposed to show," he said, knowing he'd pretty much blown his cover if anyone had been watching when he rushed to the former chief of police's aid. "Brennan," he said, shaking first Declan's hand, then Charley's.

"Declan Cavanaugh." Declan introduced himself, then nodded at Charley. "And that's Detective Randolph. You want to tell us what happened?"

"Not all that much to tell, really." What there was he had repeated several times over already, at this point he recited the words by heart.

Brennan went over the details of the event as succinctly as he could. When he finished, Charley realized that as horrible as this all was, it could also represent their first real break in the case.

Excitement vibrated through her as she asked, "You saw the shooter? You saw the guy who shot the chief? Can you describe him?" she asked, her voice growing in intensity.

Before Brennan answered, she looked at Declan and said, "We can get him together with a sketch artist and maybe we can finally start cramping this SOB's style." Her eyes shifted to Sean. "We're going to get him. I can *feel* it."

"Funny thing about that," Brennan said. "I didn't get really close, so I could be mistaken, but from where I was, the shooter looked like a woman— at least, the shooter's movements made me think that 'he' was actually a 'she,'" the undercover agent confessed.

Charley's mouth dropped open as her brain connected two stray items.

"What is it?" From his vantage point—Sean was standing directly opposite Charley—he was the first to see the startled expression cross her face.

Maybe she was forcing this—but her gut told her she was right. "Those surveillance tapes I was reviewing yesterday, the one from the restaurant where they found the last victim in the alley, it showed that teacher from the second murder, the one we previously interviewed going into the restaurant. I thought it was an odd coincidence at the time," she confessed, "but maybe it wasn't all that much of a coincidence. Maybe that teacher is our cop killer."

She knew that her sentence bordered on the ridiculous—but stranger things turned out to be true. The woman was tall, she recalled. And big boned. Strong enough, Charley thought, to be able to move the body of an average-sized man.

"What are you talking about?" Declan asked, trying to follow her line of thinking.

In her excitement, she realized that she was getting ahead of herself. Charley took a deep breath. She needed to slow down.

"The second victim was found in the parking lot of a middle school, remember?" Declan nodded as she continued, doing her best not to talk too fast. "We interviewed a teacher, a Mrs. Miller who was the only one who was at the school at the time the victim was found there." The moment she said it, things began to fall into place. "Why didn't I think of this before?" she cried.

"Think of what before? Charley, what the hell are you trying to say?" Declan asked.

"Take it from the beginning, Charley," Sean advised.

Her enthusiasm kept tripping her up. "I think that maybe we've been looking at this from entirely the wrong angle."

"I'll bite, what angle should we have been looking at this from?" Sean asked. They were now joined by an extremely worried-looking Brian. Sean put his arm around his younger brother and said, "He's going to be all right, Brian. Andrew is tougher than all of us."

"Yeah," Brian replied, his voice sounding exceedingly hollow. He turned toward Charley. "I didn't mean to interrupt. You were saying?"

Charley felt decidedly strange, airing her newly formed theory before men who'd been solving crimes since before she was born, but sometimes, the obvious was easily missed.

"That maybe the killer isn't a former police wannabe or someone who was let go or fired in disgrace. Maybe the killer is related to someone like that. A loved one of someone who became so despondent because they either washed out or were terminated that they went off the deep end or maybe even killed themselves. And this person is looking to avenge them."

She of all people should have seen that this was a possibility, Charley upbraided herself. After all, she had refused to sit out the investigation because she wanted to get justice for Matt. What if the killer, in her own twisted way, wanted the same thing? What if the killer was a woman who was looking to avenge a brother, a father, a husband or a son?

Declan realized where his partner was coming from. "We need to get back to the precinct, review the records for any former policeman or academy washout who took his own life, say in the last couple of years," he said to his father. It was a starting point, Declan thought, growing hopeful that they were finally on the right trail. "You'll let me know the second Uncle Andrew's out of surgery?" He made the request of Kendra, one of his sisters, feeling that his father and uncle had enough to cope with right now.

"Count on it," Kendra promised.

Nodding at her, he turned toward Charley. "Okay, let's go."

"I don't know how I missed this," Charley said once they were in her vehicle and peeling out of the

parking lot. "It seems so obvious now," she casti-
gated herself for the umpteenth time.

"Nobody else thought of it, either," Declan
pointed out. The reason for that was simple. "That's
because when people think serial killer, they usually think of a male behind the spree, not a woman."

Charley nodded. While serial killers were pre-
dominantly men, it was irresponsible of them to
rule out a woman.

"Obviously a mistake," Charley agreed. "Ain't
equality grand?" she murmured sarcastically, more
to herself than to Declan.

"Damn," he muttered, annoyed with himself. In
his hurry to get to the hospital as fast as possible, it
was as if he'd left his brain behind.

"What's wrong?" Charley asked, sparing him a
quick glance.

"I should have gotten that guy's cell phone number—Brennan," he interjected in case she didn't
know who he was talking about, "so we could send
him a photo of that teacher you found on the surveillance tape, see if maybe he recognizes her from
the shooting." As he said it, Declan saw the corner
of her mouth curving. Had he missed something
else? "What?"

"I already got his number." She'd obtained it as
Declan was asking his sister to notify him when his
uncle came out of surgery.

Declan could only laugh shortly. "Of course you

did." He grinned his approval. "You're turning out to be one hell of an asset, Charley."

"Is that what I am," she said innocently, "an asset?"

She was a hell of a lot more than that, he was beginning to realize. Funny how you could go through life, not realizing that something was missing until you found yourself face-to-face with it, wondering how you'd managed to go all this time without it.

Declan didn't intend to be without it any longer if he could help it. But now wasn't the time to discuss what was on his mind. They'd talk once this case was safely resolved.

"We'll talk about that later, after we get this shooter," he promised.

"Whatever you say," Charley replied. There was nothing more important to her than getting Matt's killer—and nothing more important to him and the rest of his family, she knew, than getting the person—male or female—who'd almost succeeded in wiping out the Cavanaughs' acknowledged patriarch.

"Hey, is it true?" Bobby Yu asked, hurrying over to them the moment he and Charley walked into the squad room. The tall, buff Chinese-American detective who prided himself on his martial arts proficiency, something he had been practicing since his eighth birthday, had been working with one eye on the door, waiting for Declan to appear and fill him and the others in on what was going on. Rumors were bouncing around the squad rooms like energized rubber balls.

Like them, Bobby had come in to get an early start working the case. Unlike them, he, Sanchez and Callaghan hadn't been roused in the middle of the night with an emergency phone call.

He appeared genuinely concerned as he asked, "Did the cop killer get the former chief of police?"

"The chief's been shot," Declan confirmed. "But when we left the hospital, he was in surgery."

"Then he's alive?" Sanchez asked, hope entering his eyes.

The detective quickly made the sign of the cross the way his mother had taught him to do when he was a very little boy. A hardened detective, Sanchez still took comfort and strength from the simple gesture.

"He was when we left the hospital." With Sanchez and Callaghan joining them, Declan addressed all three men. "Guys, we need to look at those surveillance tapes again, and comb through newspaper stories one more time."

"What'd we miss?" Sanchez asked.

Declan looked at the man as he answered, "That the killer might be a woman."

Callaghan's eyes widened. "You're kidding."

"I never kid about murder," Declan answered grimly, then paused for a moment, glancing in

Charley's direction. "It was Charley's idea," he told them, willingly giving credit where it was due. Then he gave them the best news so far. "There was a witness to the chief's shooting, so maybe we'll finally get this SOB whoever he or she really is."

And then he glanced at Charley. His thinking was out of sync, he realized as he said, "We need to get to the crime scene."

Having this hit so close to home had made him temporarily forget about protocol and the chain of events. He was putting last things first and vice versa.

"I wonder if they've sent out a CSI unit yet to where Andrew was ambushed?" Yu posed the question to Charley.

"I'll bet you breakfast-to-go that they have," Charley replied, hurrying to catch up to Declan. She hadn't realized until now how *really* long his legs were. "And I bet your father sent that Brennan guy back out there to work with the unit, since Brennan was there to begin with and saw it all go down."

"No bet," Declan told her, never breaking stride as he made his way to the elevator.

She was practically jogging now, but she wasn't about to complain. Declan had had a scare tonight and she completely sympathized with him. "What's the matter, Cavanaugh, don't like losing?"

Declan laughed as he hit the down button. "No,

I don't," he admitted. "You've hit the nail right on the head, Randolph."

In more ways than one, he added silently as he slanted a quick glance in her direction.

And once this was all behind them, he was going to tell her about all those ways. And do something about it.

Chapter 17

The CSI unit was already on the scene when she and Declan arrived, just as Charley had predicted. And Brennan was there, apparently waiting for them before he got started.

"You want to walk us through it?" Declan requested.

"Sure," Brennan responded, nodding a silent acknowledgment toward Charley. "That's why I'm here—but my part in this isn't going to take up much time. I was over there," he told them, pointing to the alley that had, until last night, practically been his home away from home. The undercover agent had what appeared to be the top portion of a twin mattress set that had seen better decades serving as his makeshift bed. His past couple of meals had come from the trash cans that were located aromatically close by.

Looking the area over, Charley shivered involuntarily. "No offense, but I don't think I'm looking to relocate to your part of town soon."

Brennan laughed. "None taken. And since I was most likely recorded rescuing the chief, I'm probably going to be forced to relocate myself." He shook his head, looking around the alley. "Can't say I'm really going to miss this."

"Back up," Declan said. The DEA agent looked at him questioningly. Both Declan and Charley said the key word that had caught their attention at the same time. "Recorded?"

"Well, yeah." Brennan appeared to think that was rather self-evident. "There are a number of security cameras around here." He pointed at stores on both sides of the wide street. "Not to mention the one mounted over the intersection."

Declan exchanged glances with Charley. He could see she was thinking the same thing.

Gotcha!

"Where did you say the shooter was standing?" Declan asked.

"When I heard the chief's tires squealing, he was trying to miss someone who was standing in the middle of the road."

"Had to be the shooter," Charley declared. There

was no other conclusion to be reached. "After the windshield was shot out, which way did—"

She didn't get to finish her question. The DEA agent pointed directly behind her. "I saw the shooter running in that direction. I would have followed, but it was either that or saving the chief. I went with saving the chief."

"And we're all glad you did," she agreed.

Declan was already striding back to the crime-scene investigators. "Get the names of all the stores on either side of the road and find out if they have working security cameras. If they do, I want all the footage subpoenaed," he told the lead investigator.

"What about the one over the intersection?" Brennan asked. "Seems to me that would give you the best view."

"That," Charley told him, "we have back at the station." Right in their own backyard, she thought. And they'd missed it.

But they were going to get their hands on it the minute they got back. Their first decent lead— thanks to the police chief.

Charley fervently hoped that the man would live long enough to appreciate the irony of the situation.

Finished giving his instructions to the lead CSI, Declan caught her eye and motioned for her to head toward her car. They needed to get back to the police station stat.

As he got into Charley's vehicle, Declan's phone

rang. "Cavanaugh," he snapped, yanking at his seat belt with the opposite hand. Buckling up was awkward at best.

"Tell Charley she was right," Bobby Yu said. "We found that woman she was looking for on the restaurant footage and it's the same one who worked at the middle school where our second victim turned up."

"You're sure?" Declan pressed.

"I'm looking at her likeness right now. It's her, all right. Or her identical twin sister," the detective threw in cavalierly.

"We're coming in," Declan said. Ending the call, he tucked the cell phone back into his pocket. Because he was seated, it wasn't easy.

"Who was that?" Charley asked.

Glancing down at the speedometer, she forced herself to ease her foot off the gas pedal. Tension and anticipation were causing her to press down harder. She'd already gone over the speed limit twice and although there was no traffic at this time and they were conducting a murder investigation, none of that mattered if she plowed into another vehicle or lost control of her own.

She drew in a deep breath to steady her nerves.

"Detective Yu," Declan answered her, shoving his cell phone back into his pocket for a second time. When it refused to retreat and stay put, he gave up and held it in his hand. "You were right."

Charley nodded as if she expected to hear as much. "Good to know." Then, when he didn't elaborate, she prodded, "About?"

"That teacher who was on the scene when the second victim turned up. Yu just confirmed she was on the tape, entering the restaurant where the fourth victim was found in the alley, next to the Dumpster. Correct me if I'm wrong," Declan mused, "but didn't she say that her husband had been a cop?"

So he remembered that, too. She wasn't imagining things. "That she did," Charley agreed.

Declan glanced at the speedometer. "You're going over the speed limit again," he pointed out.

Charley had a hard time not laughing. He was lucky they weren't flying. "You let me off with a warning, Officer, and I'll make it worth your while."

Declan pretended to take umbrage. "Are you trying to bribe me?"

Charley grinned at him. She was feeling really good about this. They were closing in on the killer—once brought in, they could all stop looking over their shoulder and second-guessing their every move.

"Yup."

He nodded, as if that was all he wanted to hear. "Okay, as long as I know."

Charley didn't bother stifling her laugh.

They arrived at the station, and then the squad room, a few minutes later. Yu was surprised to see them there, given that they'd been all the way across town when he'd called Declan.

"What'd you two do, fly?" he marveled, looking from Declan to Charley.

Declan slanted a glance at his partner. "Pretty much," he replied. "You got this woman's address for us?" he asked.

"Address, phone number, back history, anything you want," Yu told him proudly. He'd worked quickly, sensing they were on to something. "By the way, she's not married to a cop," he said, pausing dramatically before clarifying, "She *was* married to a cop."

"That's right, she'd said she was a widow. How did her husband die?" Charley asked.

She could feel herself growing more excited about the trail they were on. The case was gelling and could very well be wrapped up by the middle of the day.

"I looked up his file on the database," Bobby answered. "It said that his death was an accident, but I've got my doubts. Miller was being let go because someone accused him of accepting kickbacks to look the other way. There was a prostitution ring operating somewhere in the area," the detective elaborated.

"What happened to the charges?" Declan asked.

"They were dropped when Miller died—but his wife still wasn't entitled to get his pension because of the accusation."

"Which would explain why she was still working," Declan concluded.

"And why she's so angry," Charley added.

"She didn't seem angry to me," Declan said.

"The woman on that restaurant surveillance tape was not running for Miss Congeniality," Charley pointed out.

Right now, they were waiting on another surveillance tape. The one from the camera feedback that was periodically amassed in the traffic surveillance room. Declan had sent Sanchez down to get it. All the major traffic intersections had a corresponding monitor that was displaying what was going on at that specific intersection.

During the day, there were several officers seated in the room, monitoring the traffic and on the alert for any accidents and blatant traffic violations. But during the evening, there might be just one officer in the room, or, at times, none.

Such had to be the case last night, Declan surmised. But at least they had the tape.

Clearly having used the stairs and run all the way, Sanchez breathlessly presented the DVD to him.

They lost no time in loading it onto a computer.

"Son of a gun, there's the shooter," Charley cried less than ten minutes later, after having sped up the recording twice. She looked to Bobby. "Can you enlarge this?" she asked.

"Piece of cake," he told her. "Give me a couple of minutes."

He did it in one.

"It's her, all right," Charley cried, looking at the monitor.

"Find me an ADA who can get a warrant for us to search this woman's house," Declan ordered Callaghan. The detective was halfway to the door when Declan called after him, "Go see Janelle. She's the daughter of the chief of Ds. She won't ask you a hundred questions, she'll just get a judge to sign off on it."

"Do we have to wait for that warrant?" Charley asked, wanting desperately to go out and corner the woman on the tape.

As she looked back, there had been something off about the woman when they'd questioned her, but she'd chalked it up to the teacher being acquainted with the second victim.

It had all been there, in plain sight, and she'd missed it, Charley upbraided herself. She wanted to get going. There was no telling what the woman was up to at this point. She could have taken off to save herself—or she could be planning one last huge hit.

"Hell no," Declan assured her. "We're paying that docile schoolmarm a visit. Now."

* * *

They brought backup with them, but Declan instructed the officers to stay back until he gave the order. If this *was* their killer, he didn't want anything spooking her until they had her in their sights—preferably in custody, as well.

Driving up to the woman's house, Declan parked Charley's car at the curb. "You ready?" he asked Charley before he opened his door.

So ready that it was unbelievable, she thought. "Try and make me stay away," she dared him.

"Not on your life," he laughed grimly. "I know better than to get between you and something you've set your sights on."

Together they approached the front door and rang the doorbell. When no one answered, Declan tried again. When there was *still* no answer, he knocked. Or, more accurately, he pounded.

"Mrs. Miller," Declan called out. "Open the door. This is the Aurora P.D. We have a few more questions to ask you."

The door finally opened and the tall, gray-haired, heavyset woman with the round, jovial face looked from Declan to Charley.

"I talked to you before," she told them, as if that should be the end of it.

"Yes, you did," Charley agreed brightly, doing her best to put the woman at ease. People could be tripped up more easily if they were at ease. "But we need to ask you a few more questions."

"I've already told you everything I know about that poor officer," Donna Miller protested.

Watching the woman's face carefully, Charley said, "This is about your husband."

Suspicion immediately entered the small, close-set brown eyes. "What about him?"

Charley had taken over this segment. Declan let her, hoping it would built up some sort of rapport. "We're here to clear up a few things that we found on his record."

The last of the smile faded from the woman's face as she opened the door farther. "Come on in," she said flatly.

When they did, the woman surprised them by suddenly grabbing Charley and pulling her over, using her as a human shield. Donna Miller had a small but lethal pistol in her hand that she'd pulled out of her skirt pocket. She pressed the muzzle against Charley's temple, her intent very clear.

Declan instantly pulled out his own weapon, aiming it at the middle-school teacher.

"Drop your gun, Detective," Donna Miller snapped. "Drop it or I'll blow a hole in her head this minute."

"You don't want to do that," Declan said, keeping his voice low, calm.

"Oh, but I do," Mrs. Miller contradicted. "I want

to blow a hole into every damn cop in this city. You killed my Howard and it's only right that you pay for it. That you *all* pay for it. All he ever wanted was to be one of you," she accused. "You took that away from him. He was so depressed, he killed himself. That was *your* fault," she screamed wildly, then temporarily regained control over herself. "It's only right that you pay for it. Now put your gun down— or watch her die right in front of you! Your choice," she concluded malevolently.

"Don't do it, Declan," Charley cried, her eyes riveted to the weapon in his hand. "You put your gun down, she'll kill us both."

"You're probably right," he agreed. "But I can't risk it." His eyes shifted to the woman's. "I'm putting it down," he told her, slowly lowering his weapon. "Let her go."

"God, but you *are* stupid," Donna Miller laughed, shifting the muzzle away from Charley's temple and pointing it straight at Declan. "You should have listened to your girlfriend here."

Charley knew she had only a split second before the teacher fired. With a wild yell to throw the other woman off, Charley drove her elbow into the woman's considerable rib cage as hard as she could.

A guttural scream of pain and anger pierced the air as the woman attacked Charley. They struggled for possession of the weapon amid a flood of curses the middle-school teacher heaped on her.

Declan ran to the fighting women, attempting to pull them apart. It was almost impossible at first, but he finally managed to pull the teacher off Charley at the same moment that Mrs. Miller's pistol discharged.

The next moment, Declan wrenched the weapon away from her.

"Here, take this," he told Charley, shoving the weapon into her hands. The next moment, before she could say anything to him, she watched in horror as Declan sank to his knees in front of her.

Blood was pouring out from his left side.

The teacher began to lunge toward her, wanting to seize her chance. Charley pointed the weapon at her. "One more move and I'll shoot you dead right here."

"You can't do that, you're a cop," the teacher taunted.

"Want to bet your life on that one?" Charley challenged coldly. "Just take one more step. *Please* take one more step."

For the first time, the teacher appeared to be terrified.

Grabbing the woman's arms roughly, Charley handcuffed her hands behind her back, running the cuff's link through a breakfront filled with knick-knacks that were badly in need of a dusting.

Done, she quickly turned toward Declan. Charley frantically stripped off her shirt in order to have something to try to stem the flow of blood before he bled out at her feet.

Barely conscious and lying on the floor, Declan looked up at her and said weakly, "This…is no…place…to have…your way…with…me, Charley."

Tears were streaming down her face and she didn't try to wipe them away. Something far more important was happening for her to be worried about her vanity. One hand pressing down on his wound, with her shirt between his skin and her hand, Charley had her phone in the other.

"Officer down," she cried into her cell when someone picked up on the other end. "Officer down! I need a bus sent to 15073 Magnolia. *Now!*" she fairly screamed into the phone.

She dropped the phone and used both hands to press down on his wound. Her shirt was now all but completely red.

"Stay with me, Declan. Stay with me!" she pleaded. "Open your eyes and stay with me!"

"You're wasting your time," the teacher laughed. "He's dead."

"The second he is, so are you," Charley promised the woman just as Yu, Callaghan, Sanchez and the rest of the backup team broke in through the front door.

Charley barely heard them. She was far too busy begging Declan to open his eyes for her.

Chapter 18

She never let go of his hand.

When the paramedics arrived, Charley insisted on riding in the ambulance with him.

Though he was unconscious, she held Declan's hand tightly the entire trip to the hospital, afraid that if she let go of his hand, he would let go of life.

So she held on.

And prayed.

The moment the paramedics pushed Declan's gurney through the E.R. doors, the physician on duty took over. Though every fiber of her system resisted, she had to release Declan's hand.

"We have to operate and you can't be in the O.R.," the nurse told her gently.

Nodding, Charley released his hand, but not before she bent over him, brushing a kiss to his forehead. "You come back to me, you hear? I'll never forgive you if you don't. Never," she repeated hoarsely.

"There's a room right over there where you can wait for the surgeon to come out and talk to you," the nurse told her, pointing to a room down the hall.

"I'll wait right here," Charley insisted, leaning against the wall some ten steps away from the swinging doors the orderly and physician had just gone through with Declan.

"A Cavanaugh tradition," the nurse said with a weary sigh, apparently knowing that to argue with her was pointless. "You'll fit right in."

If Declan died, she would never fit in anywhere again, Charley couldn't help thinking.

And then, before she realized what was happening, Charley found herself engulfed by off-duty police officers and detectives, all of whom shared her pain several dozen times over. Declan's family, both immediate and extended, all congregated around her.

Still reeling from the shock of seeing Declan go down before her eyes, Charley looked at the people around her, stunned.

"Haven't you gone home yet?" she asked, and then a cold chill ran down her back. "How's the chief?" she asked Sean, the Cavanaugh standing closest to her.

Had the unthinkable happened? Had Andrew Cavanaugh become that damn serial killer's latest and last victim? Was that why most of his family was still here at the hospital?

"Doctor said the surgery was a success and that that lucky son of a gun cheated death again. There's every indication he's going to be even better than new," a very relieved Rose told her, joining her brother-in-law. "But why are you here?" Andrew's wife asked. "And what are you doing wearing an orderly's shirt?"

She'd forgotten that one of the paramedics had lent her an extra shirt that was in the rig. "I used mine to try to stop Declan from bleeding out. We got her, sir," she said, turning toward the chief of detectives who had made his way to her.

"Her?" he repeated quizzically.

Charley nodded. "The killer turned out to be a woman," she told him. "Donna Miller. Her husband killed himself after he was dismissed from the police department in disgrace—he was about to be investigated as a dirty cop. Something snapped inside of her and she started killing the people she felt were responsible for her husband's termination."

"She confessed?" Brian asked.

"In a manner of speaking. It was more bragging than confessing. She thought she was going to kill us both." Her voice cracked and Charley paused for a moment. "It'll all be in my report, sir," she told him after a beat. Charley felt incredibly exhausted and nervously hopeful at the same time.

"That's one report I want to read personally," Brian said. "How did Declan get hurt?"

Charley pressed her lips together before beginning. Reliving the events was difficult for her. It was going to take time for the images she'd witnessed to stop haunting her.

"She had a gun. It went off while he was trying to get it from her."

Brian looked at her knowingly. "Something tells me that there's more to that than you're saying."

There was, but she just wasn't up to talking about it yet. "It'll be in the report, sir," she promised again.

He nodded, accepting her excuse. "In the meantime," he asked kindly, "is there anything any of us can get you?"

"A miracle would be nice," Charley said, thinking of Declan.

Brian nodded as he slipped his arm around his wife, Lila, who'd silently come up to join them. The smile he gave Charley was one of encouragement. "It's already on order," he promised her. "By the way, Detective," he said to Charley as she was about to return to her post by the swinging doors, "your brother would have been very proud of you."

"My brother?" she echoed as if she didn't know who the chief was referring to.

"Yes. Sergeant Holt. You did him proud."

"You knew?" she asked him, stunned that he'd allowed her to continue the investigation if he knew her connection.

In response, Brian smiled at her. "I'm the chief of Ds, Charley. I know everything," he cracked, tongue in cheek.

"Well, *almost* everything, dear," Lila told him, patting her husband's chest in a lovingly tolerant manner.

Charley didn't know what to say. Fortunately, no one was waiting for her to respond. But she flashed the chief a grateful smile that was not lost on Brian.

It was, perhaps, the longest two hours Charley had ever been forced to endure in her life. Every minute seemed to lethargically drag itself by, limping into the past.

Each time she saw the doors that led into the O.R. as well as several other restricted-access rooms swing open, her heart began to pound and her pulse spiked.

But the hospital personnel who came and went through those doors had no news of Declan or how his surgery was progressing, and then her heart would plummet down to her toes.

After two long, endless hours of this, Charley wasn't sure just how much more she could handle.

Concerned about how pale and haunted she looked, Sean walked up to her and took her hand. The iciness startled him.

"Your hand's ice-cold," he said. Then he rubbed it a little to return circulation to it. He treated her the way he treated all his children, with thoughtful kindness. "He'll be all right," Sean assured her, then added with a kindly smile, "After all, his life's finally coming together. Declan now has everything to live for. That'll help pull him through."

She nodded in response, appreciating what Declan's father was attempting to do, but knowing that sometimes positive thinking wasn't enough. If it had been, then she would have been able to dig Matt out of that emotional abyss he'd allowed himself to sink into and who knew? Maybe that would have been enough to save her brother and he wouldn't have provided that killer with a target.

The second the surgeon walked through the swinging doors, his surgical mask hanging about his neck, Charley snapped to attention. She was the first one to reach him.

"Doctor?"

Charley couldn't bring herself to say anything beyond that, just his title. Every fiber in her being was silently pleading with the man to tell her what she wanted to hear.

When he did, she felt so giddy with relief, for a moment she was afraid that her knees were going to buckle. She grasped someone's arm—Sean's?— to keep from sinking to the floor.

"He's young, he's strong and the surgery went well. The next twenty-four hours are crucial, but there's every indication that he'll pull through," he told the sea of faces that were all focused on him, listening to his every word.

A murmur went up around the surgeon that sounded very much like a cheer.

The E.R. nurse who had attempted to herd them into waiting rooms when Andrew had arrived appeared again, asking them, "*Now* will you people disperse or at least clear my hallway?"

They were far more accommodating now that there was hope.

But as they drifted into several of the opened surgical waiting areas, Charley asked the nurse, "Which room will you be putting Declan Cavanaugh into?"

The woman paused before the closest computer, typing something on the keyboard. The monitor left its sleep mode and became bright.

"Room 320," she said. "But he's not going to be there for another hour. The patient's in Recovery now."

"I'll wait," Charley replied.

"Why don't you go home and come back?" Brian

suggested. She looked as if she'd been through hell and he didn't doubt that she had. "I'll have someone drive you."

But Charley shook her head. "Right now, this *is* home," she told him just before she headed for the bank of elevators that were located a few feet to the left of the swinging doors.

She allowed herself to cry in the elevator.

Declan was going to be all right.

Declan struggled to open his eyes, somehow aware that there was a wall of pain shimmering just out of reach, waiting to begin closing in around him the moment he became fully conscious. His mind alternated between half-formed dreams he couldn't quite make out and the scenario he remembered just before the world crashed into darkness around him while he was riding a red-hot flame comprised solely of pain.

What he recalled, beyond the burning pain, was someone holding his hand tightly, telling him over and over again that he wasn't allowed to die.

Charley.

Charley had been the one who had forbidden him to die, he realized. Charley's voice had pulled him back from the brink of oblivion even as he was set to relinquish his own slender hold on life.

Declan forced open his eyes and saw the

slumped, sleeping figure sitting in the chair that was pulled up as closely as possible to his bed.

Charley.

She was still holding his hand, he realized, as if that was the last barrier between him and the jagged pain that was waiting to collapse in on him.

"Charley?"

The moment she heard the raspy whisper, her eyes flew open even as her heart began pounding wildly.

"Declan?" She moved to the edge of her chair, taking his hand in both of hers.

"What's left of me," he answered. "What are you doing here?"

"Making sure you don't skip out on me," she quipped. Her face clouded over. "Don't you ever, ever do that to me again," she warned, doing her best to sound angry. She couldn't quite pull it off.

"Hey, are those tears?" Declan asked, trying to focus.

"No, I just sprang a leak," she snapped, brushing the tears away. But it was a useless endeavor. The tears, born of relief, just refused to abate.

"You should do something about that," Declan told her.

"Yeah," she mumbled, still holding on to his hand, adding flippantly, "First thing in the morning."

"Good," he exhaled. Then, as events began to

return to him, Declan asked, "How's Andrew? The surgery, did it—"

"The chief's doing well. He came through the surgery like a trooper. A full recovery is expected," she summarized, her eyes all but devouring him.

She'd gotten regular reports about the chief's progress in the past eighteen hours from Declan's family. Different members came and went from the room, checking on Declan—and her.

"You've been here the whole time?" Declan asked her.

She shrugged, trying to dismiss her part in any of this. All that mattered was Declan. "Seemed like the place to be. I'd better go and tell everyone you're awake," she said, beginning to rise.

But this time it was Declan who was holding *her* hand, keeping her from moving. She looked at him quizzically.

"Not just yet," he told her. His throat felt so dry, it was hard getting the words to come out. "I want to tell you something."

She sank back down in the chair, a new nervousness undulating through her. She tried to brace herself—but couldn't.

"Okay," Charley said slowly.

She had no idea what he was about to say. Was he going to say something like it was her fault that he'd gotten shot? That if he hadn't tried to pull that woman off her, the gun wouldn't have discharged, nearly ending his life?

"When I opened my eyes just now and saw you there, I realized something."

"What?" she whispered, afraid of hearing what he might have to say, that he felt she was getting too close to him, that now that the case was over, he was going to put in for another partner.

Her breath stood still as she waited for him to speak.

"I realized," he said slowly, because uttering each word really hurt, but he wanted to get this out before he drifted off to sleep again, "that I wanted to go on doing that."

"Opening your eyes?" she guessed.

"Yeah, that—and seeing you there when I did," he said.

"So you don't want to get rid of me?" she asked, trying not to sound as happy as she really was. She failed.

"Get rid of you?" he repeated, confused. Where would she get an idea like that? "I want to marry you."

Charley's mouth dropped open. When she finally found her voice, she told Declan, "Okay, you're still delirious."

"No," he contradicted, "maybe for the first time, I'm clearheaded."

"Except for the anesthesia and the pain medication they're pumping through your veins," she cracked drolly.

"That's not it," he argued. "I'm going to feel the same way tomorrow, and the day after that, and the day after that. I had an epiphany just before I was shot."

"Did you, now?" she asked, humoring him. It was wonderful just to hear his voice, she couldn't help thinking.

"I realized, when that crazy woman had a gun to your head, that I didn't want to lose you. That I loved you and I wanted a chance to prove it to you. I'm going to keep on asking you to marry me, Charley, until I wear you down and you say yes."

"This must be your lucky day because I'm pretty worn down already," she said. And then she said one more word to make it official. "Yes."

Declan grinned. He would have cheered if he wasn't so weak.

"You're going to have to lean over," he told Charley, his voice beginning to fade as sleep began to slowly overtake him again, "so I can kiss you because I can't sit up yet."

She smiled, feeling another wave of tears coming on. "I guess I can do that," she whispered.

And she could.

Epilogue

"Get that thing away from me, I'm not using a wheelchair," Andrew declared, waving away the wheelchair that Brian brought into his hospital room.

It was time to go home. He had signed all the papers, jumped through all the hoops and was more than ready to leave the hospital behind him as quickly as was humanly possible.

But he was *not* going to do that leaving being pushed around in a wheelchair like some damn invalid, Andrew thought angrily.

It was the principle of the thing more than the fact that he felt in tip-top shape. Because he didn't.

The former Chief of Police still felt rather weak, certainly weaker than he would have either wanted or liked.

But he would be damned if he was going to let on or have anyone guess that at the moment, if he were challenged to a wrestling match by a two-month-old kitten, there was a fifty-fifty chance that the kitten might just win. As long as he took slow, steady steps and perhaps linked his arm cavalierly through Rose's—as much for support as for emotional comfort—no one would suspect that he had seen far better days as far as his stamina and his strength went.

"It's hospital policy, dear," Rose told him in a low-key, soothing voice.

"I don't care if it's written on two tablets of stone, I'm leaving this place on my own power," Andrew declared, glaring at the wheelchair.

"There are rules, Andrew," Brian told him calmly. "You don't want to set a bad example for the next generation by breaking rules, now, do you? Declan's being released, too. He's already out in the hallway, waiting for you. *He's* sitting out there in a wheelchair."

"Good for him," Andrew grumbled, then threw up his hands. "Oh, okay," he agreed, lowering himself into the hated chair in question. "Anything to get me out of here."

"Knew you'd come around sooner or later," Brian

said with satisfaction. "Especially if we told you that Declan was following hospital protocol and was sitting in a wheelchair."

"What do you mean 'if'?" Andrew asked suspiciously.

"Same thing worked on Declan," Rose told him as Brian wheeled her husband out of the room. "You Cavanaugh boys are so predictable—no offense, Brian."

He laughed as he wheeled his brother out. "None taken."

"What are all these cars doing out here?" Andrew asked as they approached his house.

"Sitting from the looks of it," Brian answered innocently, bringing the CRV to a stop in Andrew's driveway.

The poor joke didn't fool or distract Andrew. There was only one reason why there would be so many cars parked along his street. Or why, he suddenly realized, whoever was driving Declan's car had come here rather than gone on to Declan's home.

"Don't tell me that you're throwing me a welcome home party," Andrew said, looking more stunned than happy. He turned toward his wife. "I love you more each day, but you and I both know you can't cook for more than five people at a time."

"Which is why I had help," Rose told him, unfazed by his display of doubt regarding her culinary abilities. "And just so you know, it takes five of us to replace one of you. Now let's get you out of the car so you can say hi to your family."

"You don't have a damn wheelchair hiding someplace to spring on me, do you?" Andrew asked suspiciously, his eyes sweeping up and down along the street.

"Afraid not. Just my shoulder to lean on if you need to." She got out and came around to his side of the vehicle.

Andrew got out more slowly than he was happy about. Even so, he knew he was lucky to be alive. "I can do that," he told her with a flirtatious smile.

"Then let's go. Oh, and by the way, that new branch of the family you tracked down for your dad just before you went and got shot, scaring the life out of me?"

"What about them?" he asked.

"They're here. Sean drove over to the next town and invited them, too."

Andrew nodded his approval as he made his way up the walk with steps smaller than he was happy about. "Shows a lot of promise, Sean does."

"You sure you're up to this?" Declan asked Charley as she pulled up her car beside Andrew's. One of Andrew's sons had made sure that there were two spaces directly in front of the house just for them so that neither man had to do very much walking. "We can turn around and go home."

"And miss the chance of witnessing the great unveiling?" she scoffed. "Not likely."

"Great unveiling?" he repeated, then asked, "What great unveiling?"

She waited for him to get out on his own, knowing what his pride was like. "Of more Cavanaughs, that branch Andrew tracked down and talked to just before he was shot."

Declan laughed, shaking his head as he put his arm around her shoulders, silently accepting her help. "Just what the world needs. More Cavanaughs."

"Yeah," she agreed as they began the journey to Andrew's front door, "it does."

And very soon, she thought in delight, her grin widening, she was going to be part of them.

Life felt really, really wonderful.

* * * * *

A sneaky peek at next month...

INTRIGUE...

BREATHTAKING ROMANTIC SUSPENSE

My wish list for next month's titles...

In stores from 21st February 2014:

❏ The Girl Next Door – Cynthia Eden

& Rocky Mountain Rescue – Cindi Myers

❏ Snowed In – Cassie Miles

& The Secret of Cherokee Cove – Paula Graves

❏ Bridal Jeopardy – Rebecca York

& The Prosecutor – Adrienne Giordano

Romantic Suspense

❏ Deadly Hunter – Rachel Lee

Available at WHSmith, Tesco, Asda, Eason, Amazon and Apple

Just can't wait?

0214/46

MILLS & BOON® Book Club

Join the Mills & Boon Book Club

Want to read more **Intrigue** books?
We're offering you **2 more** absolutely **FREE!**

We'll also treat you to these fabulous extras:

- **Exclusive offers and much more!**
- **FREE home delivery**
- **FREE books and gifts with our special rewards scheme**

Get your free books now!

visit www.millsandboon.co.uk/bookclub
or call Customer Relations on 020 8288 2888

Discover more romance at

www.millsandboon.co.uk

- WIN great prizes in our exclusive competitions
- BUY new titles before they hit the shops
- BROWSE new books and REVIEW your favourites
- SAVE on new books with the Mills & Boon® Bookclub™
- DISCOVER new authors

PLUS, to chat about your favourite reads, get the latest news and find special offers:

- Find us on facebook.com/millsandboon
- Follow us on twitter.com/millsandboonuk
- Sign up to our newsletter at millsandboon.co.uk

'EB_SD